Brandy and the Banshees
by
M. D. Mascaro

Sleep O babe, for the red bee hums the silent twilight's
fall,
Aoibheall * from the grey rock comes, to wrap the
world in thrall.
A leanbhan O, my child, my joy, my love my heart's
desire,
The crickets sing you lullaby, beside the dying fire.

The Gartan Mother's Lullaby
Seosamh MacCathmhaoil, 1904

* Aoibheall
 (pronounced evil, Queen of the Northern Fairies)

TABLE OF CONTENTS

Chapter 1 –

And The Band Does Not Play On

"Would you put that freaking thing out, Farrell?" I yelled. "How can I sing if I'm coughing my ass off ?"

I watched Farrell finish splicing the synthesizer wires together with duct tape. Crap! If I hadn't seen Ron's cymbals fall and slice them in two I'd have never believed it. What sucked even more was that our regular bass player, Los, had bagged out last minute with a nasty stomach virus and, to top it all off, Stan had made the wrong turn over the bridge with the equipment truck and we were setting up mad late to begin with. This gig had a black cloud hanging over it and it wasn't only from Farrell's stinky, fat cigar.

Farrell slid the rank looking brown carcass from his lips like a wet, necrotic pickle. The smirk on his face said he was enjoying pushing my buttons, and I suspected that was one of the more spiteful reasons for his new vice. That, plus he was an asshole and thought it looked cool.

"Chick singers...," he taunted, sucking on it like fast little kisses at the tip, spewing the stinking smoke thicker just to piss me off.

"Mother...!" I leapt over a road beaten equipment case and a spaghetti tangle of wires, managing to land a soft kick against his hip as he twisted his butt away from the tip of my Doc Martins.

"Knock it off you two!" shouted Stan, pulling his equipment case closer towards himself, just in case we were going to continue.

But we weren't getting into it tonight. We were opening for Enemy Fire and, in about an hour, record company gurus were going to start pouring in like vodka on New Year's. Even Farrell knew to let it go.

I pulled the neckline of my dress back down over my shoulders and returned all the décolleté holes to their appropriate place. My get up was Stan's sexist idea of how the lead female vocalist had to dress to front the band. (He *hated* my burgundy pixie cut!) I would rather have been in jeans so I could have beaten the crap out of Farrell. But the dress had cut outs all over linked with a rhinestone chain, and the hemline, even pulled down, barely covered my ass as I bent down to continue trashing a case for my mike. Not much fighting anyone could do in that get up. Thanks a crap load, Lady Gaga and J-Lo. If White Noise wasn't the only garage band in town headed out of the garage I would've told Stan to shove it.

"You know, Brandy, you need to ditch the tough-girl act. Let your hair grow..."

"The only act I do is the one you see when I'm on stage, Stan. And I play it because," I made air quotes, "it's 'your band, your rules'. Off stage I'm still Brandy Connor...."

"Yeah, yeah. Raised with five fighting-Irish brothers...I know the drill."

"An' the Little People, Stan. Don't be forgettin' the Little People," threw in Farrell with a mock Irish brogue.

Farrell was hinting at an old private joke between us, one that had never been funny to begin with, but I let it slide. Everyone was on edge. Enemy Fire, was mega hot right now, and if our drummer, Ron, hadn't roomed with Darren Wilde, Enemy's even hotter lead singer, we'd have been playing some dumpy bar in Jersey instead of a top, three-floor, NYC lounge soon to be teeming with agents and deal makers. Not that I was fooling myself or anything. I knew they were mostly there for Darren, but there was that "anything can happen" feeling in the air. I yanked my dress into place again, took a deep breath and decided that the night would go much better if I just chilled and pretended that Farrell didn't exist. We all went back to setting up.

I helped Stan untangle his wire case and was setting up my mike stand when a cold breeze moved past me from nowhere. It creeped me out. I was shuddering and rubbing my forearms when I glanced up across the long, narrow room and saw a good looking guy in a long black leather coat step through the front entrance. *Calm down, girl. It's just a draft from someone opening the door.*

"Hey, Bran!" Ron called over his high-hat. "Get me a beer, will ya'?"

"Me too." chimed Stan.

Stan and Ron were the only two in the band who were legal and *I* had to go get the booze. I nodded my good sport nod, kicked off my boots, slipped on the red, platform Demonias that I wore on stage, and started towards the bar with the fake ID my friend Celeste had hooked me up with.

Two feet from the bar, the wind moved past me again. I shot a quick glance up front; the door was closed. Odd. I was usually high-blood-pressure hot before a gig but tonight I was freezing my ass off. Nerves? Or the cooling effect of a crappy stage dress full of holes?

Leather Coat Dude was sitting at the bar. He could be from Sony or, judging from the wear spots up close, maybe a sub-label. I slid my ass onto the stool next to his and shot him a little smile. I wasn't flirting. I'm not into that. This was business. But, evidently, my lack of experience with eyelash batting wasn't going to serve me well; he didn't even nod my way but tossed his head back to slug down a shot, called for the bartender, and waved two fingers over the glass to indicate more.

"Three Buds," I said to the bartender when he finished pouring the Jameson's. I flashed Leather Coat Dude another little weak smile.

There was something about him that drew me in. Something vaguely familiar. Had he been to our gigs before? Was he an agent? A scout? Actually, I was hoping he was a complete nobody so I could relax, not imagining every face in the crowd belonging to someone who could change my future. "*Chill!*" I could tell myself all night. "*You were wrong about the leather coat dude.*"

"Ummm...you here to see 'EnemyFire'?" Duh. Great opening; mention the other band. But the double shot seemed to have his complete attention.

"Lord Almighty! Why don't they stop the

4

noise?" He sounded agitated. And Irish. His accent was thick as Bailey's.

"They're just tuning up. They'll stop in a minute."

"No. Not them." He rolled his eyes around the room as if following a fly's path and, when his gaze passed me, he paused and smiled a little. "I'm sorry. Guess it's the jet lag. Been a bit jumpy. Here! Barkeep! Another!"

He knocked back the contents of the fat glass and slammed it on the counter in one smooth motion but his hand was shaking as he held it up for a refill. I tried to change the subject.

"So, you're from Ireland?"

No. Botswana, Brandy. I was really racking up the duhs.

His face brightened a bit. "Just arrived yesterday from Dublin. It's me birthday today." He took half a slug of his refill, put down the glass, and grabbed his head. "God! All that screamin'!" He rubbed his temples and stared down into the amber depths of his drink.

Black Leather Coat Dude was just some drunken wacko on drugs. I triangled the beers with two hands and made a beeline for the stage calling "Happy birthday!" over my shoulder.

Our first set opened to a typically sparse New York early crowd - five people including the crazy Irish guy and the bartender. It wasn't encouraging. All I wanted was for us to get a shot at being seen by someone more important than a few boozing office workers unwinding from a grey, windowless day stuck in a cubicle on the 27th floor.

"Hey, everybody! Welcome to Smash Cats! We're White Noise and this is one of our originals, 'White Line Riding', written by our own Dirk Farrell and, yours truly, Brandy Connor!" I pronounced his name "Dork" just to aggravate him. I couldn't get *that* chill.

Farrell hit the first few notes loud and smooth on the guitar as Stan ran a dark, driving riff under them. I started to sway through the intro. Jordan, Los's replacement, pulled his bass close to his crotch like a lover and pulled the strings so hard that the notes reverberated right between my bare legs. And didn't stop.

Feedback! Shit!

I looked over my shoulder. Farrell was moving his mike. Jordan was backing off of his. Stan shoved his amp over about seven inches with his boot. But the sound still didn't stop. It only got louder, higher. Operatic feedback. It sounded like singing.

Like *her* singing.

I felt the blood drain from my face and the chill I'd been feeling all night moved over my body like a pair of cold, dead hands. Feeling like a wuss, I covered my ears. It was that bad.

"Pull the friggin' plug!" I screamed. The high-pitched whine reached up another octave and impossibly more. As hard as I was pressing on my ears, I could still hear it.   In another minute I was sure we'd be in dog range and either the pain would stop or my eardrums would bleed and I'd be deaf. Either way, I figured I'd be out of this misery soon.

Ron reached behind him for the wire that led to the strip where most of the equipment was plugged in and gave a good yank. The room went quiet and I breathed a sigh of relief. Then a wind kicked up. *Inside the room.* Stan's crib sheets blew off of the top of his amp and whipped around the stage. Ron's cymbals shivered back and forth. And this time, as the whine started again, I knew exactly what it was.

It was the same sick, singing whine that I'd heard the night mom died.

This wasn't feedback. It was the banshee.

As the wind turned into a mist, the sweet white face I remembered coalesced and hung before me. Her eyes were at once beautiful and sorrowful, her expression full of longing. She floated in front of me for a moment and I got the creepy sensation that she wanted to stay with me. It froze my heart and the flow of time turned into a thick, slow, syrup with everything else in the room spinning as if in a centrifuge.

When The Lady finally flew off over my head, I exhaled, thinking everything would calm down. But the noise and wind only grew fiercer.

"Pull out the amp!" screamed Stan, kicking his again.

"I did!" Ron held up the power strip's plug.

"Can you see her?" I shouted at Farrell.

"See what? What the hell is going on?" he said, scrabbling after Stan's music sheets as they flew across the sticky platform.

Maybe the guys hadn't seen the face that lunged at me from the ectoplasmic whirlwind but

I knew they heard the terrible, screeching lament. It crescendoed even higher than before. Now I wasn't the only one holding my ears.

As glasses exploded behind the bar, a second banshee appeared. She swooped in a low arc across the room, rising up in front of me just like mom's banshee. Only the face before me was hideous. I felt myself teeter a bit as I stared into cadaverous, sunken cheeks and a gaping, shapeless hole that passed for her mouth. I got the distinct feeling that she was sizing me up with the red, rheumy eyes that met mine not three inches from my nose. If mom's banshee had frozen my heart, this one took an ice pick to it and shattered it.

At that moment, the glass rack above the bar came crashing down, and the bartender, a tough looking bald dude who must have seen combat at some point in his life, ducked down shouting "Hit the dirt!" My heart slammed as I jumped three steps back and almost fell into Ron's drum kit. Ron fell backwards into the space between the stage and the wall. Jordan dove behind one of the speakers as Stan jumped off stage right and ducked into the men's room. Farrell, damn his unpredictable ass, ran up, grabbed my arm, and tried pulling me back further but I whipped around, stuck out my foot, and tripped him. He went careening ass over teakettle off the stage, landing under one of the empty tables in the front row. I didn't need his help; I knew all about the *bean sí* and I wasn't afraid for myself.

Then, in a cold, sudden instant, the wind

and the wailing soprano voices from hell stopped dead. And I was the only one still standing.

From my vantage point at the front, the place looked like the aftermath of a combination bar fight and earthquake. It was also desolate. Where was everyone?

One-by-one they crept out like bugs: Ron crawled up from behind his drum kit, Jordan scuttled across the stage's grimy rug, Stan's head peeked out tentatively from the bathroom door. The bartender and Farrell picked themselves up from the floor, flicking glass splinters off their clothes.

Only Leather Coat Dude remained immobile, his head bent limply over his drink, his nose in the glass, drowned and dead in two ounces of Irish whiskey.

*

Gram's big, open kitchen was warm and as butter yellow as the autumn leaves of the gingko tree outside her window. I had almost finished peeling potatoes and was rolling a smooth round one around in my hands absentmindedly when its cold whiteness suddenly unnerved me. I threw it hastily into the waiting bowl of ice water, splashing all over the table.

"What's wrong, lass? Yeh seem a bit out o' sorts today? Didn't your important... what do yeh call it again?"

"Gig," I offered.

"Yes, that's it. Didn't it go well?" Gram

calmly mopped up the spill from across the table with a white linen towel. Having raised six boys of her own, any mess that covered less than half the floor did not perturb her.

"There was a problem. Um...someone got sick and the gig got cancelled that's all."

"Aw.   Too bad child.   Too bad.   But," Gram's face brightened and the whole kitchen seemed to glow, "there'll be other gigs."

Dad's voice boomed from the other room. I bent back to get a better view of him through the archway that led to Gram's parlor.   He was comfortably perched on his favorite throne, Grandma's threadbare but beloved Queen Anne chair.

"And then the archers breached the walls! Waterford fell and the Normans tore in and killed a great many people! The blood, it is said, ran like streams down the streets."   Dad was telling another one of his Irish history stories to my five brothers: Michael and Patrick, the twins; Sean, the linebacker; Brian, the engineering student; and Dylan, xylophone player par excellence in the Dover High School Marching Band. (Name wise, we are not a very creative family.) Most of them were splitting their attention between Dad, beer, and a football game going on softly on the TV in the corner of the room.   Only Dylan, my "baby" brother, just two years my junior at fourteen, sat at his feet in the rapt attention my father thrived on. Dad was in great form, gesticulating and pulling out his best Irish accent for effect.

"He's always fancied himself a seanchaí," noted Gram, lifting her eyes from her work for just a moment.

"Yes, but I think he's stealing from Frank Delaney," I replied, "a real seanchaí is supposed to make up his own stories, isn't he?"

"It's all about tradition. Stories are overheard and handed down from generation to generation and from storyteller to storyteller but everyone puts their own color on it." She chopped another potato methodically. "I don't think Frank Delaney would mind."

Truthfully, much as I loved helping Gram, I envied Dylan's seat at my dad's feet. Dad's tales of Irish history were just one item in a long list of interests my brother and I shared. Mom had always said we were "of a mind". I'd even gotten my nickname from him. Bridget Anne, the full given name that my parents called me when I was in trouble (which was often), was shortened to Bran because Dylan couldn't pronounce all three syllables any more than he could accurately say Dylan. He referred to himself as Dee and we were together so often that it was Bran and Dee that ran together into one homogenous word. When I learned that it was a nickname, I never introduced myself with my "church name" again, even though Dad was not entirely pleased at having a daughter who insisted on using the name of an alcoholic beverage.

Dad's voice broke the little bubble of thoughts of brighter days as he shouted something about a head rolling in the gutter.

"Where," I asked Gram cautiously, "did he learn stories about things like faeries and leprechauns?"

Until last night, I hadn't thought of those tales much since Mum died, and I'd been glad to forget them. Stories about supernatural creatures were one thing that set me apart from my scrappy brothers and made me feel like a wuss. They gave me night terrors but, when I'd wake up screaming or get frightened by something I'd seen or heard, Dad's idea of comfort was to tell me I had "the sight", which only made me feel worse.

"Oh, I don't wonder he got some stories about the Little People from books too. Not from Delaney, o' course. Folklore collections and the like. And from listening to your grandfather, may god rest his soul. Lots of places."

"Hmmmm." I wanted to know more but Gram was a simple woman and I knew I'd have to be more direct before I could find out what I wanted to know.

"And even, banshees? Those stories too? Did Grandpa ever tell stories about banshees?"

"Well," said Gram lifting her eyes to heaven and crossing herself, "that'd be another thing in this family."

I sat up stiff and straight, hanging on Gram's words in anticipation. I knew that banshees were often attached to old Irish families and the Connors were descended from quite an ancient line indeed.

"But we best not be speakin' o' that, child," she said in a tone that told me the subject was off limits.

Hopes deflated, I stripped off the last few pieces of skin on the spud I was working on, slid it into the water, pulled another gritty globe from the bag, and headed to the sink to wash it. The faucet whistled a little as the water rushed out so I pushed down on the lever to curb the flow. But the whistling sound continued and the memories it evoked made me shudder. I slammed down on the handle with an audible smack, shutting it completely. Still the shrill noise continued insidiously, rising to a louder, higher pitch like a tight little shriek caught at the back of someone's throat. I recalled Leather Coat Dude and what happened when Mother died and held my breath, immobile, afraid to turn around, afraid not to.

No, I thought, no! Not Gram! Not here and especially not now. Just last night I'd watched as the paramedics had lifted Coat Dude's dead body from the bar, his face frozen in a grimace of terror. I did not want to turn and see that look on my dear Gram's face. But I had to; maybe this time I could help.

I wheeled around to face the table where Gram had been sitting. She wasn't there.

"Gram?" My own voice was a shrieking gasp.

"What's wrong, child? Y'er jumpier than a dancer at Lughnasa!"

I turned full circle to see Gram at the other end of her long kitchen, standing by the stove with the still whistling tea kettle in her hands.

*

We got back from Gram's house after eleven. I kicked off my jeans, threw myself onto the bed and fell into a fitful sleep. It was close to midnight when the cell phone rang in the charger next to my bed. I leaned over, fumbled for it, and opened it up with the wire still dangling.

"Y'lo," I managed.

"Brandy! It's me, Farrell."

Click! No need to have that idiot adding to my nightmares.

I'd already dozed off again when the phone went off in my hand; startled, I dumped it on the floor. The activity of untangling myself from the covers to grab it out of my sneaker made me a bit more lucid.

"Listen, Farrell, it's bad enough I have to work with you but..."

"Brandy, shut up for a minute and listen. I'm right outside your window. Open the..."

Click. Crap! What the hell was that asshole doing here at this hour?   I ran to the window and drew back the soft lace curtains that mom had brought from a visit to Ireland so many years ago when she'd still had hopes of turning me into a little ballerina. There stood Farrell, just behind the spiny bushes that were supposed to offer some protection for my first floor bedroom. I made wild faces at him through the glass, pointing to the right where the gate was and basically mouthing "Get the hell out of here!"

Farrell was crossing his hands over and over in front of him in a "no way" gesture, shaking his head in a manner that told me the stubborn idiot was going to stay out there all night.

The worn metal window latches were thick with paint and squeaked a little as I turned them slowly and lifted the creaky sash about a foot.

"What the hell are you doing here!" My head was near the sill and I whispered just loudly enough – I hoped – for my brothers upstairs not to hear.

"Listen, Brandy, I have to talk with you. I tried calling you all day...."

"My batteries were dead and the phone was home, and now I'm really glad it was. Now go home." Farrell stuck his hand through the bushes and reached over the sill just as I slammed the sash down.

"Aggggggggggggggggggggh! Ow wow ow!"

He was jumping and hopping up and down like Riverdance all over the yard, holding his bruised hand by the wrist and flapping it in the air. I yanked the old window open so hard the sash slammed up, throwing chips of paint into the room and shaking the walls around me. *Great*, I thought, *that helps*. I glanced at the ceiling an instant before I stuck my head out the window.

"Shhhhhh! Farrell! Shush up! If my brothers hear you..." I pointed up to the floor above.

Too late. I heard someone shouting upstairs. Then a green flash sailed past my window and I would have thought that it was Green Lantern dropping from the sky had I not recognized the Notre Dame pajamas that my brother Sean had been lounging in all evening. He landed on his feet and lunged at Farrell like a middle linebacker - which he was - tackling him

15

to the ground.

"You son of a bitch!"

I heard heavy feet stomping down the stairs as I started to clamber over the sill to save Farrell's life. The hedges scratched my stomach right through my T-shirt and I rolled onto the ground about five feet away from them with my panties hanging out just as all the outside lights went on. The next minute I barely missed being crushed by Patrick who came flying off the porch steps in his bare feet.

"I'll help you Sean!"

The dogpile began. Patrick threw himself on Sean and Farrell; I leapt onto Patrick's back with one hand while simultaneously trying to yank down a wedgie with the other.

"Let him go! Leave him alone! He wasn't doing anything...."

Much as I hated Farrell I didn't want to see him critically injured, nor did I want my brothers to be arraigned for manslaughter. I pulled on the neck of Sean's shirt but kept getting tossed off onto the ground by random flailing legs. The neighbor's dogs started to kick up a fuss.

"May the curse of Mary Malone and her nine blind illegitimate children chase you so far over the hills of damnation that the Lord himself can't find you with a telescope!" Father's voice boomed over the fracas, shouting Irish curses as he threw himself into the melee, grabbing one of Farrell's legs, trying to pull him out of the tangle and off the property.

The neighbors' lights went on. Farrell was

screaming something about a law suit. I tried to separate them all, pulling at shirts, shorts, anything I could get my hands on and falling down numerous times in the process, especially since Dad kept throwing me off balance by grabbing me with his free hand whenever he could and shouting "Get in your room and put on some clothes!"

Then, in the corner of my eye I spied Mike and Brian rounding the corner with baseball bats as Dylan leapt over the front porch railing with a ping pong paddle.

"Get away from my sister, Dork Farrell!" shouted Dylan, reminding the entire neighborhood why Dirk had always insisted on using his last name.

It was time for desperate measures.

"Stop it! Stop it! All of you!" I screamed, standing between Farrell and the newcomers. "I CALLED Farrell and ASKED him to come tonight. This is all my fault! I MADE him come here!"

Sean lifted his head. Dad and Patrick almost let go of Farrell's legs. Everyone stood mid-motion. Mike and Brian dropped the bats. Dylan's ping pong paddle froze over his head. They all looked at me, then at Dad.

"Bridget Anne Connor! Go to your room!" said Dad in an uh-oh-you'd-better-listen voice. "Boys! Help me escort your sister's guest to the door."

Each of my older brothers grabbed an arm or a leg and Dad led them to the front gate with Dylan bringing up the rear. I looked back just in time to see them fling Farrell over the fence into the hedges on the other side. Rubbing the scratches on my stomach, I winced in empathy.

Back in my bedroom I quickly crawled under the covers. If I knew Dad - and I did - I was in for a lecture that only unconsciousness could protect me from. The door creaked open in less than a minute.

"Don't be feigning sleep, Bridget Anne. You were brawling in the yard in your underwear not a minute ago, young lady. Sit up and explain yourself. Didn't you disgrace yourself enough with that boy, and now you're inviting him to your bedroom?" He pulled my desk chair over to the bed and sat down. "I thought we made a deal so you could get your chance with the band but....you've betrayed my trust." He sounded angry, hurt, and embarrassed all at once. Anything potentially involving his little girl and sex embarrassed him. "Did...did anything happen here tonight?"

I pushed off the blanket, sat up and shot a look outside, unable to make eye contact.

"It's not what you think. Not at all. I....I needed to talk with him. Something happened last night."

My father's bushy brows raised so high that I thought they were going to cover his bald spot.

"Something? *Last* night? What's this something? Do I even want to know, Bridget Anne?"

Dad's face was beet red; I knew what he was thinking. Just this past summer, he had caught me and Farrell in a heavy make out session. Farrell's hands were up under my blouse and we were twisted and tangled together on the sofa like a package of Twizzlers left out in the sun. Dad chased him out, and I was grounded for a month and had to promise to do an entire semester of Sean's comp papers just to have him cover for me so I could sneak out to rehearsals. Ostensibly, I spent a lot of time that summer watching Sean's scrimmages.

"Nothing like THAT happened, Dad," I offered immediately. "Something happened at the gig."

"Bridget Anne, I told you it was a bad idea singing with that gang of losers! They sound like a bunch of constipated dogs! I told you to join the church choir and give the voice God gave you to..."

"Somebody died."   I figured that would stop Dad in his tracks, and it did.

"Died? Sweet Jesus! What happened? Did one of the fools electrocute himself?"

"No, no, it wasn't anybody in the band. Some guy came in while we were still setting up. He was a little weird. I think he had a heart attack."

The window was letting in the cool night air. I pulled a folded quilt up from the foot of the bed, shook it open and wrapped it around me. Dad got up slowly, walked over to the window, stuck his head out, perused the yard, shut it, locked it, and returned to the chair. He rubbed his hands on his knees thoughtfully for a few moments before he spoke.

"So you didn't get your big break," he said

finally.

"Hardly. We didn't even get to play. By the time the paramedics were done and the ambulance had left, it was time to pack it in and let the other band set up. It suck... stunk."

"You do recall our little deal, don't you?"

"Oh, Dad, please don't make me quit the band! We'll get another chance soon, I'm sure of it! I broke up with Farrell like you said, I only see him at rehearsals now like I promised, I've been doing good in school..."

Part of that was true. I was doing great in school and I wasn't seeing Farrell, but I had never broken up with him. It was the other way around.

"Bridget Anne, Bridget Anne. When will you ever learn? I don't want you wasting your energies with that bunch of apes. You pleaded with me all summer and I said you could go back to work with the band until this big chance of yours was done, and now it's done and so are you! No more band! And - thank the lord! - no more of that loser Dirk Farrell!" He raised his eyes heavenward. "May he be tormented by itching without nails for scratching! Now get to sleep!"

Chapter 2 - The Connor Curse

"Ah, yes! Hearts, stars and harseshoes! Clovers and blue moons! Pots o' gold and rainbows! And our lord and savior, Jesus Christ. We thank yeh for this breakfast!"

Dad frowned as Patrick spilled out his unconventional blessing along with a fake brogue and a copious stream of Lucky Charms.

"Mmmmmm..." he continued, pouring more sugar on the already sweetened cereal. "Magic'lly delicious!"

"And where's the pot o' gold for your dentist bills?" said Father, pulling the sugar bowl away from his spoon.

It was Monday morning and the seven of us were seated together as Dad had decreed was to be "our custom". With Michael and Patrick working, Brian's robotics club, Sean playing college football, and Dylan and I involved in after-school musical ventures (Dylan's the more "respectable" high school marching band), dinner together during the week was sometimes impossible, so breakfast was "family time". In other words, get your butt up early whether you have to or not.

I was picking at a chemical-flavored "lite" yogurt when the phone sounded on the kitchen counter. Brian had it programmed to play "Irish Eyes". He bent backwards to get a look at the caller ID.

"No phone at family breakfast," said Dad,

not even looking up from his oatmeal.

"It's Gram," said Brian.

Father wiped his mouth and jumped up from his chair. Grams never called, much less at breakfast. We all watched him as he pulled the phone from the cradle.

"Top o' the mornin' to yeh, mother!" He was teasing her because Grams always said that no *real* Irishman would use that expression.

Gram's voice was uncustomarily animated. We couldn't hear what she was saying but the pace of her speech carried across the room, especially since she was speaking so loudly that Dad had to hold the phone away from his ear.

"The police?" Dad exclaimed. "What for?"

All eyes locked on him. Patrick dripped milk down his shirt because he was trying to eat and watch at the same time.

"Aidan's boy? Sweet Jesus! But why would the police be calling you about the goings on in Ireland?"

More mice noises from the receiver across the table.

"What? The poor lad! Where was he then?"

Bzzz squeak yada yakka yakka.

"Ah, well, that's typical. Where is he now?"

The squawking from the handset continued.

"Well, we'll need to call a funeral director then."

Patrick missed his mouth, spilling Lucky

Charms onto his lap. At the same time, my cell phone buzzed in my skirt pocket against my hip bone and made me jump. I snuck a look at the text message under the table. It was from Farrell.

> im in st clares tx a lot i was trying 2 help u
> ded man had yr name on him

I felt light-headed. Farrell was in the hospital and Leather Coat Dude had been looking for me? I sank down in my chair and stopped eating. Could things possibly get any weirder?

They were about to.

"Oh go on with you, Mother! The Curse indeed! Didn't I have five strapping boys?"

Meepa meepa blahda bzzzz.

"Well, Michael and Patrick are fine and don't you be worrying yourself with some silly old curse. Now just settle down, take a Tylenol, and I'll call you from work if I can get the afternoon off."

Dad hung up the phone and turned to face five dropped jaws that immediately started to move with questions.

"Who's Aidan?"

"Why did the police call Gram?"

"Why are you calling the funeral parlor?"

"What curse?"

"Why's Gram worried about me and Patrick?"

"Settle down all of you!" shouted Father over all the commotion. "Settle down and I'll explain!"

He took his place again at the head of the table.

"One of your cousins from Ireland passed away."

"Which one?"

"Why'd they call Gram?"

"I want to hear about the curse!"

"Yeah, me too!"

"Yeah! Tell us about the curse!"

"Quiet!" Dad's voice boomed and everyone hushed. "My Uncle Aidan's only remaining son just passed away and you're all excited about some stupid curse?"

Everyone shut up for a moment but then Dylan pressed on.

"Aw, c'mon Dad. None of us have even met our cousins in Ireland. It's not like we're not sorry or anything but we all want to know about the curse. Please?"

Dylan was the "baby" and, since mom died, Dad could hardly resist any of his requests.

"How did he die, Dad?" I ventured.

"Big commotion of some sort on Saturday night. Bar fight it seems. In New York City."

The blood drained from my face.

"Do you know the name of the bar?"

"Shut up, Bran! Who cares about the name of the bar? We all want to hear about the curse," interrupted Brian.

"I haven't the faintest idea, sweetie, now

24

let me be tellin' the story before it gets too late."

Dad was already slipping into the brogue that was the signal for story time. "As some o' yeh may have heard mention, there's a bit of a feud in the family. When Grandfather Peter died, lord rest his soul, he hadn't spoken a word to his sister, Maggie, in Ireland for over forty years. Well, what yeh may not have heard is the reason why."

I didn't know which story I wanted to hear more, Dad's or Farrell's. I glanced up anxiously at the corny, google-eyed-cat kitchen clock with the swinging tail. No matter what, we were all likely to be late to our respective destinations.

"Your great-grandparents, Meghan and John Connor, had your great aunt, Maggie, when they were quite young and livin' on the end of a rasher. Your great grandmother was of a frail constitution to begin with and the birth all but killed 'er. She had no luck holdin' onto babies ever after and the sad pair lost many a child before they gave up hope that Maggie would ever have any brothers or sisters or, if god blessed them with a pregnancy that might come to term, a mother who survived to raise them.

"Maggie was quite a homely child. Gawky and freckled and....ah! truth be told she had a face like a harse's arse! Why, the poor child's prettiest feature was a blemish! She had a small, heart-shaped mark over her lip that her mother called 'God's Kiss' and she'd give the poor child a sweet peck on it every night before bed. It's a sad thing indeed when your loveliest feature is a mole! Her only savin' grace was her bright red hair, but even

25

that betrayed her, for when she was walkin' ahead in the street and turned to show her uncomely features, well, it hardly fit a stranger's expectation. Maggie got used to surprised expressions from others and taunts from the children in the village, but she was Meghan and John's only child and they loved and fussed over her nonetheless.

"Well, as time heals all wounds, so time healed whatever ailed your great grandmother and, when she was close to her thirties, she gave birth to three more children in as many years: your great-uncle, Aidan, your grandfather, Peter, and your great aunt, Molly. Everyone was delighted except, as yeh might guess, Great Aunt Maggie.

"As yeh can well imagine, Maggie, now at an even gawkier adolescent age, did not want competition for the attention of the only ones from whom she could count on it. To make matters worse, your great-aunt, Molly, was a real beauty, right out of the cradle! And Peter and Aidan were handsome, curly-haired boys as well, so Maggie spent most of her time after their births in a jealous snit. There was no consolin' her. She'd had all of her parents' attentions too long and she wasn't willin' to let the little ones have so much as a diaper change in peace.

"Well, the family went on this way for a good long while. In time, Maggie came to a begrudging tolerance of her siblings but her disposition gradually set into one as sour as her looks. Of course, this only made things worse for her social life and, by the time she'd reached her late 20's, she hadn't had one suitor nor many friends to speak of. It was about that time that she had the encounter with the banshee."

My yogurt suddenly threatened to reappear.

"Now I've told yeh some of the legends of the banshee, the messenger who announces death in the old Irish families. And yeh know the tales of the insulted banshee and the story of the mark of the five fingers and the theft of the banshee's comb. All o' that is traditional Irish folklore. But the Connor family's tale is – shall we say - non-traditional, if yeh get my meanin'.

"Maggie was comin' home very late from church in the fall. She liked to make a show o' bein' overly pious y'know. I don't know if she was curryin' favor with the lord where she missed the favor of her fellow men or if she was just tryin' to one-up the whole family in the one thing she could certainly excel at. She always prayed the hardest, sang the loudest and stayed the longest.

"Well, she was makin' her way past a cold field of grey stone just after sunset when she saw some snow on a slab in the distance. Snow? She hadn't seen any snow fall and why would it be fallin' on only one spot in the field?

"Maggie snuck closer for a look, thinkin' maybe one of the sheep was out but as she drew closer she near fainted. It was an old, shriveled banshee just settin' there on the rock, combin' her long white hair in the gatherin' dusk, no doubt getting' ready to pay a local visit. The frail old gal was using the loveliest of little combs and it looked of a gold color with the last grey light reflectin' off a precious stone or two.

"Now Maggie was neither particularly brave nor particularly adventurous, and she didn't have a greed for riches either, but one thing she did want - and badly - was attention. She'd heard the stories of the dangers in stealing a banshee's comb but what a tale she'd have to tell if she could possess it! She'd be a legend in the parish for a long time to come. She figured she'd be called up to tell her story like old man Malone who had a run in with a kelpie in the river. She might even be invited to parties!

"Emboldened by these thoughts, Maggie snuck up light as a fairy behind the ancient vision who sat unawares in her relaxation. And whist! Maggie snatched the comb right from the banshee's hand as she lifted it over her head for the start of another long stroke.

"Now it isn't impossible hard to steal a banshee's comb, but keepin' it is a horse of a different color. A banshee's quick and fierce when she wants what's hers. But Maggie - poor, gawky, lanky thing - had long thin legs and much experience runnin' home to escape the jeers of the other children. She managed make it to the cottage in a dash. Quick as a bunny, she let herself in and slammed the door shut in the nick o' time! She run up to her room, tossed the comb on her dresser, and jumped into bed shiverin' with the covers over her head.

"Now, as yeh might guess, that was hardly the end of it. From the legends yeh all know the banshee will plague any soul who's got what's hers, and plague this banshee did. She howled outside Maggie's window with near every dog in the parish barking straight along with her lamentations. Maggie's folks couldn't hear the banshee but the entire village heard the dogs and everyone knew somethin' evil was afoot.

"The next mornin' dawned and Maggie stayed in bed all day, too afeared from the night's chase and all the howlin' racket. After survivin' another night of screamin' and barkin', Maggie's curiosity took hold and she began to stare at the comb, examinin' its knot work and its prettiness. Gold it was indeed, with three stones set in it, bright blue and green and a royal purple like the sky and trees and the deep shadows of the forest where the Little People reign.

"Later that day, Great Aunt Maggie confided her plight to your great great grandmother. She showed her the fine little comb too but the wise old dame wouldn't touch it. 'Place the cursed thing on the window sill with a pair of iron tongs you stupid girl!' she said, crossing herself, 'Why even with the tongs, you're in grave danger. I heard a tale of a poor lad shoved the comb back outside under his door, and the tongs come back to 'im a lump of twisted metal. But you've got to try! If your luck holds the banshee will scoop it up and leave you be!'

"But Maggie took no heed. She felt she'd gone too far already and determined to sit out the wails until the banshee tired and gave it up at last. She who had never felt the confidence of her own power turned it all in her mind to a struggle, a battle if yeh will, between her and the banshee, and she was determined to win.

"Well, after three howlin' nights, no harms come to her or her own and Maggie's so comfortable with the situation she's almost taken to playin' with the comb. And here's where her story parts with all legend. At the crack of dawn of the third day ...."

Father stopped. He always did this. Whenever he was getting to the punch line he'd stop as if to test us, to tease us, to see if we were listening, to enjoy hearing us beg him to continue.

"And what, Dad?" said Dylan, almost always the most attentive.

"WHAT?" My voice came out surprisingly loud. "What's all this got to do with our dead cousin?"

Dad's eyes were on the swishing tail cat clock.

"The 'what' will have to wait until suppertime, I'm going to miss my train and I have to ask my boss for time off to help attend to your cousin's arrangements, so being late today would be especially bad."

The demeanor of the seanchaí was gone. The accent was gone. Good ol' Dad was back to reality and on his way to work. He gathered his things with Dylan trailing after him pleading for more and shouting: "But I won't be home for supper! I have band practice!"

*

Right after Dad left the table with Dylan, I raced to my room and changed into jeans and sneakers.

"Brandy, would you hurry up! I'm going to be late for class and the prof is a real pain in the ass!" Sean hollered through my door. I always hitched a ride with him on the days he was heading out for an early class at college. It was a great way to lessen the amount of weekly lectures I had to hear from Dad.

"Bran! I swear! I'll leave without you."

I flew out the door almost as fast as Sean flew down the roads but, by the time we were two blocks away from Dover High School, the funeral procession to the main entrance had already started.

"Can I *please* let you off here," he said right before the corner of Garrison. "If I turn here I'll save a lot of time."

"Sure," I replied, trying to sound a little perturbed so he wouldn't suspect anything. He knew I usually hated walking in front of all the asshole rapper wannabees that gathered in clusters along the way trying to sneak smokes. But, this time, I had no intention of passing them. It was about a mile and a half to St. Clare's hospital and I'd changed into my sneakers for a reason.

I lugged my backpack out of the front seat, slammed the door, and took about six slow steps towards school before I shot a look over my shoulder. Sean's car was halfway down Garrison. I stopped a minute, took a few more lame steps forward, ground my toe nervously in some gravel on the sidewalk, then turned on my heels and double backed down Grace just as Carlos was crawling up the line of traffic in his Dad's old yellow Corolla.

Jumping off the curb, I ran over and tapped his window frantically.

"Los! Los! Open up!"

He slammed on the brakes so hard the car behind him lurched to a stop two inches from his bumper even at that slow speed. The parent in the car gave him the finger but he didn't see it because he was leaning over to open the door for me. I slid in the front seat, scooting way down into "drive-by shooting" position.

"'Tsup, Bran?"

"Hang a U-ey," I replied scooting even lower down.

"Wha'?"

"Just do it," I snapped. "Cut down Berkshire. Let's get out of here."

"Whoa! Miss Crabface's star English student gonna' cut honors? What's up with that?"

"Shut up. Didja hear Farrell is in the hospital?"

"No way!"

"Way! He's in St. Clare's. And I have to talk to him."

"Shit. I promised my dad I wasn't gonna cut anymore, Brandy," he said with a grin as he did a quick turn. "Yeah, riiiiight."

Sneakers or no, I didn't want to walk if I didn't have to and Los's supersonic driving meant I was going to get some answers that much faster.

"What's up with Farrell? And tell me

about the gig, too. Jordan told me there was a murder."

"Ahhh...he's full of it. I heard the paramedics say it was natural causes."

"Yeah, whatever, but I guess I still missed a lot of excitement by getting the shits this weekend."

Driving on 46 against the eastbound morning rush hour traffic, we would be in the parking lot of the hospital in less than five minutes but that was enough time to explain what little I knew about the death of Leather Coat Dude and everything I knew about Farrell's injuries.

"Lemme get this straight," Los said. "Your brothers beat Farrell to a pulp and hospitalized him and you are going to see him, why? He'll probably go into a loony rage. 'Get her away from me! Get her away from me!'" Los screamed and twisted the wheel as he spoke causing the car to veer left and right on the highway and someone in the oncoming traffic to lay on his horn. It suddenly occurred to me that we had seat belt laws and I fastened the buckle.

"Nah! I don't think so. He texted me this morning. He's got something to tell me."

"Yeah, like: 'Here's the name of my lawyer and I'm taking out a restraining order against you and your family.'"

The lobby of St. Clare's was pleasant enough considering it was a hospital. It was bright and well lit with the usual cheery gift shop at the entrance. I had three bucks on me and I went in and bought Farrell a couple of Snickers.

The drab elevator plodded up to the third floor and I braced myself for a vision of traction, plaster, and a possible full body cast. I was surprised to see Farrell sitting up reading *Guitar* magazine with nary a bandage in sight.

"Hey dude!" he addressed Los, punching the air in his direction and ignoring me. "I can't believe you made the sacrifice of cutting class to see me!"

I thought he was busting Los before I realized that the latter comment was addressed to me. Farrell knew I loved English class in spite of Crabface.

"Yeah, well. I felt bad about the fight..." I said sheepishly, noting a linear bruise just above his knuckles where I'd slammed the window down.

"Don't front, Bran, you want to know about the dead guy."

I scowled. "Okay, yeah, but I do feel bad that my brothers landed you here."

Farrell broke out in a hysterical laugh. "Look!" He pulled on his gown, indicating some scratches on his neck and a black and blue mark on his left arm. "This is about the worst of it. Your brothers can be assholes but they're not homicidal and they fight fair. The guys were taking some lame pot shots in the dog pile and, when I was pinned down, Sean pulled his punches."

"Sure didn't sound like that to me. You were screaming."

"All for effect, Bran. I'm not stupid enough

34

to shout 'You're hitting me like a girl!' when I can't defend myself."

"Well then, what's up with the hospital room, man?   Establishing a fake court case?" suggested Los. I glowered at him.

"Appendicitis."

"What?"

"I had an attack last night when I got home. At first I *did* think I had internal injuries – your brother Sean weighs a ton - but then I started puking my guts up this morning and they rushed me here for tests. I'm getting operated on in a couple hours."

"Oh." I said in a small voice. "Sorry."

"Yeah. Thanks." There was only a hint of sarcasm.

I bit my inner lip and shifted around nervously for a moment as Carlos launched into a vivid description of his own appendectomy. He pulled up his oversized white jersey and yanked down his already hanging-off-his-ass jeans to show Farrell the scar. I had a clear view of his designer boxers. Los was the only guy in the band who dressed like he belonged in a gang.

"So," Farrell said finally, "I guess you're wondering why I texted you this morning."

"Yeah, well, it's not every day your name turns up in a dead man's pocket."

"And that's where it was too.   The paramedics were hauling the body onto the stretcher when this piece of paper fell out of his coat. No one saw it so I grabbed it off the floor. Before I caught up with the EMTs, I glanced down and saw your Dad's name and your address on the paper. Another Connor, too. Someone named 'Kathleen' in Jersey City."

"Grams! That's my grandmother! Oh god!" I smacked my head. Now I was absolutely certain. Coat Dude had to be the dead cousin Grams had called about. As cold as the hospital room was, it suddenly got much, much colder. I thought of the terrible face of the second banshee at the club and felt light-headed. Now I was more anxious to hear about the curse than my brothers.

But first I had to faint. I don't know whether it was the too-tiny bit of yukky breakfast yogurt or the fear of pursuit by a supernatural demon from hell. Probably both. But, next thing I knew, I was sitting in a retro molded plastic chair with my head between my legs and a nurse hanging over me asking me if I was diabetic.

*

Los and I never made it back to school after the hospital. We went to Hot Topic at the mall and ate Chinese at the food court. I was still feeling queasy and only picked at my lo mein. I made it home as hungry for food as I was for the end of Dad's story.

Our family had supper worked out so that whoever was home earliest, usually me or Dylan, would cook. Everyone was grateful when Dylan had band practice because all he ever made was cardboard-crusted frozen pizza and my older brothers frequently bribed me to co-opt his turn. Tonight was definitely going to be my night.

As soon as I got in, I grabbed some cream of mushroom soup from the cupboard and started to defrost chicken in the micro. Cooking almost took my mind off of everything but, when I cut into a fat, white onion the tears instantly poured down my face, not all of them from the onion. The last bit was almost chopped when I stopped mid-slice. Through my own sniffles, I thought I heard faint sobbing from the direction of the bedroom.

The timer on the TV in my room screwed up again, I thought, wiping my eyes with the back of my sleeve. I glanced at the swishy-cat clock. Ten to four. *It's the end of a soap opera. Stop the nonsense and get a grip.*

I placed the onions in a pan of heated oil and the sizzle drowned out all sounds, real or imaginary. When everything was simmering, I went to the living room to read.

It was October and sunset was coming earlier. I hadn't gotten through a full chapter of my book when the light grew dim. I walked to the opposite end of the room to turn on the floor lamp and sank into the big recliner next to it. That end of the room was closest to my bedroom and, as I settled down, I heard the sobbing again.

Taking a deep breath, I stood up and cautiously tiptoed down the hall. Even though I always pull my door tight behind me when I leave, the door was ajar about an inch. I leaned my head close to the jamb. The weeping was definitely coming from inside, soft and muffled.

I knew it was The Lady.

I had first heard the banshee's sobs

through my own the summer night that mom went to the hospital for what I knew was the last time. At fourteen, I had no idea how I was going to survive without her. It was just after sundown, and I was lying on my bed crying as quietly as it's possible to cry when your heart is breaking. A pillow and my stuffed Jack Skellington doll were pressed over my head so that no one else could hear me, and I had lifted the pillow for a breath, stifling my sobs for just a moment. It was in that silent moment that I first heard the banshee's mourning wail.

I remembered turning over and seeing her on the window sill, just able to make out her shape against the greying sky outside. I felt a chill of fright but I'd heard enough about the banshee to know that she wasn't there to harm me. The banshee announces death in some old Irish families and, after mom's long bout with breast cancer, there was little surprise for me there. Some say the banshees are the souls of lovely maidens who'd been taken from the earth before their time. Some claim they are the souls of professional keeners, old women hired to sit and wail at funerals who took their calling beyond the grave. Mom's banshee was definitely the maiden variety. Her long hair fell around her shoulders and trailed past the sill in a spill of pale silver onto the ground. Her gown was moonlight colored, with a soft glow like a will o' the wisp. She was very beautiful.

Oddly comforted by her company, I had watched The Lady for I-don't-know-how long because I fell asleep. The next morning she was gone, and so was my mum.

Months later, I told Dad about it, and he said he felt good about my having seen her. He said a visit from a family banshee was like those visits you get at the funeral parlor from people you haven't seen in years but who still care about you nonetheless.

I stood quietly now near the doorway. And this time I was really afraid. When Mum died I'd known who the banshee was crying for. Now, with the memory of red, rheumy eyes still fresh, I swallowed hard and lightly touched the door; it swung open just enough for me to peek in. Mom's banshee was there in plain view on the sill.

Cautiously, morbidly curious, I took a light step into my room. The spectre looked up and motioned for me to come closer. My arms went all goose bumps. This was way too freaky. Still, if it was my time, running back down the hall wasn't going to change that, and if it wasn't my time, well, I felt obligated to find out whose it was.

"Are you crying for....my cousin?" The words came out a whisper, and I still didn't know the poor kid's name.

The Lady shook her head softly, covered her face with her hands, and I heard a distant voice.

"I cry for the children of Mary O'Donnell! The Connor Curse has come to these shores and more will perish till she be doneeeeeeeee!"

Her voice trailed off into the saddest keening. The slight thump of excitement that had propelled my legs through the door turned into a jackhammer in my chest.

"Who's going to die? Why? What's the Connor Curse?" My words sounded small and weak.

SLAM! The kitchen door banged open and I heard Dylan shouting:

"Bran? You home, Bran? I got out of band practice early! Where are you?"

In the second I turned from the window, the banshee was gone.

*

By the time supper came, my stomach was growling so loudly I couldn't have heard an entire pack of banshees over the sound. I was still upset but my hunger was stronger than my emotions and I tore into my chicken thigh like a savage.

"So Dad," Dylan piped as soon as the last bit of bread was passed around and the final few teaspoons of gravy were being sopped from everyone's plate, "let's have the end of Great Aunt Maggie's story now! You left us on the morning of the third day with Maggie drooling over the comb and the tale was taking a twist."

"Fill up the coffee pot, then. I'll be waiting for it while I tell you the rest."

Dylan hopped up obediently with Brian voicing his usual grumble about getting a Keurig befoe Dad went on.

"Well, where was I?" It was a rhetorical question, Dad never forgot where he ended a story. Or his Irish accent.

"Ah, yes! It was the crack of dawn on the third mornin' and our Maggie was emboldened. To her mind, the banshee's cries seemed to be weakenin'. She had held the comb in her hands many times by now and was none the worse for it. Her grandmothers' warnin' about keepin' it seemed like nothin' more than an old wives' tale.

"Well, when the first honey-gold rays of sun cracked through her window on that fateful day, Maggie awoke rested, havin' lost much of her fear. She felt bold and cheered and confident about somethin' for the first time in her life. The banshee had quieted some with the light, and yer great aunt took it as a sign she was winnin'. She was gonna have an excitin' story to tell and the proof of it right in her hands.

"She rose softly from her bed and padded over to the dresser, lookin' down at the glimmerin' symbol of her victory, nervously gigglin' a bit in satisfaction. The banshee's wail was wanin' and Maggie felt the way she was sure a pretty girl felt when she'd got a hold of another lass's fella. She was the winner. She had bested the banshee.

"She lifted the comb in her hand and ran her fingers around its rich design, over the little, glitterin' stones. It was hers. She'd keep the comb. Nay, she thought! She'd *wear* the comb in her own bright hair, and when it attracted comment, as it certainly would, she'd tell her story and watch the wonder on peoples' faces. She'd be the object of attention the like of which she hadn't known since the three little usurpers to the household throne had joined her so many years ago.

"Now, no one ever in the history of Irish time has ever placed the banshee's comb in their own hair. Most legends tell of men findin' it, and no rakehell youth or old bald pate is gonna be wantin' to snatch the comb for anythin' more than sport and a good bar story. Maggie, on the other hand, was a not-so-pretty girl with a very pretty item, somethin' a princess might wear, somethin' she was not like to see again much less own in her lifetime. Well, when she touched the first tangle with the comb the lock went slack and bright like a string of stars had shimmered down from heaven. A few strokes and her hair was a copper waterfall streamin' across her shoulders. Ah, but that wasn't the end there, oh no!

"A fairie glamour seemed to come over Maggie. She studied her plain features in the mirror. Was it her imagination or did she look....different? All her life she'd known that questioning the looking glass was an exercise in self-torture; the same, hard, angular jaw, the same flat, snubbed nose always answered back mockingly. She was used to her plainness and never spent much time in front of a mirror so, at first, she thought it was just wishful thinkin' and an unfamiliarity with her own face.

"But then yer great aunt wove the comb into her hair and set it in tight. That instant, the banshee's wailin' ceased completely and the dogs went silent. The birds were singin' in the trees and it was like it was the first time Maggie heard 'em, so great a relief come over her from the quiet. When she looked up in the mirror again, she was sure there was a change. Her dim blue eyes had a new sparkle and her features looked softer. Maggie blushed, thinkin' it was mere pride that made her glow. For once in her life, she felt victory and it tasted sweet.

"She went down to family breakfast for the first time in two days. To them that always loved her she was never plain or ugly but they noticed a difference straight off.

"'Feelin' better, love?' her mother said.

"Great Grandfather John pulled her chair out next to him and patted the seat.

"'There's my girl! Yeh must've caught a chill walkin' home so late from church the other night. Come set here close to the fire.'

"Your grandfather and his brother, Uncle Aidan, and pretty little Molly, all asked after her health as well and all agreed on how bright her cheeks seemed and how well she was looking. Only your great great grandmother, Mary, kept her peace. She'd not mentioned a word about the banshee to the family, not wantin' to worry them and hopin' that Maggie would come to her senses and give up the comb. When Maggie turned and Mary caught sight of the thing in her hair, she clutched her heart at the evil of it and fell down in a cold faint at the table. For the rest of the day, all eyes were off yer great aunt as the doctor was fetched and the family rushed about in a state.

"In the afternoon, Maggie was left alone with her grandmother while her father went to the fields to try to make up for a lost mornin', and her mum ran to town to fetch some herbs the doctor had recommended. When her gram fell asleep, Maggie went to her own room to check the comb's effects once more in the mirror. For sure there were some changes, small but noticeable changes. Her lashes seemed longer and the worst of her freckles were beginnin' to fade..

"'I'll just tell folks I've takin' to usin' lemons to clear the skin,' she thought as she smoothed her hands over her cheeks.

"It was near sunset and she hadn't heard the banshee all day. To be sure, she figured she'd seen the last of her. But then a great cry rose from her grandmother's room and Maggie went flyin' up the stairs to the sounds of the poor woman screamin'. She took the steps by twos but the cries ceased before she reached the door, and when she threw it open she found her grandmother lyin' there pale as milk with her mouth and eyes open and the old banshee settin' by the headboard.

"Yer great aunt stood frozen. She thought of givin' the comb back then and there but she knew her own life was at stake if she did. She hadn't forgotten the warnin' about the tongs, yeh see, so she fixed to fetch them.

"'Ww...wait! Let me have Gram back and I'll give yeh the comb,' she offered. 'I'll go downstairs to the fire and....'

"Well, the banshee just sat there laughin'. 'Too late,' says she, 'too late!' and her laughter just threw hatred into Maggie who had already determined that the comb would protect her from mockery.

"'Then, if ye'll be keepin' my grandmother's soul, I shall keep the comb!' she spat defiantly.

"And the banshee just laughed the louder. 'The Lord has your grandmother's soul for her time had come.'

"Tears of mournin' and anger began to pour down Maggie's cheeks. 'Well, then, I shall still keep the comb anyway for it does her no good, and your laughter makes me the more determined that it should be mine.'

"'Yes, yeh shall keep the comb, Maggie Connor, but know this: as much happiness as the comb may bring you, it will bring down sorrow on the Connor family tenfold. I have sat and mourned with your kin since the Danann walked the earth and you pay me with theft and disregard. For this, I break my peace with you and yours. And from this day forward know this: Any male child born to yer father's line will be cut down before he takes a breath past his twenty-first year. All shall suffer to see young lads wasted in the prime of life, for when the last Connor of John Connor of Sligo dies, then my soul will be free and I will have no more duty to you and yours, and no more need of my comb.'

"Well, Maggie took the banshee's words as an angry threat, denyin' their power to herself because it was the comfortable thing to do. Furthermore, with her offer to return the comb rejected, it seemed to her that there was nothing she could do. So she put it all out of her head as best she could, enchanted by her own face in the mirror growing more beautiful every day.

"And so it went that, after Mary's funeral, Maggie left home. Even at the funeral, so many

45

eyes were fixed on her that a few near forgot their purpose and ignored their respects. Maggie knew that she was changin' in a way that would be hard to explain to a village of superstitious folk and, not wantin' to be accused of witchcraft, she took up her suitcase and went off down the road, never to be seen in the county again."

Chapter 3 - Bat Shit Crazy

"So, how did anyone find out about all of this if old Mary died and Maggie left?" Brian our engineering major and ever the logical one, always found the gaps in a story.

"Well, I'm gettin' to that. After Maggie leaves, your great-uncle, Aidan, marries. Him and his bride, Maureen, have a healthy baby boy right off and then two girls and another boy child, bang all in a row. Well, when the first boy child is just three and a half, he's found drowned in a well down the road with no explainin' how he's gone out of the house. Six months later, his newborn baby brother, who seems a strapping lad, dies in his sleep.

"Needless to say, the family is all beside themselves. Such a wailin' and a cryin' as yeh never heard and your great grandmother sayin' the family is cursed and all of 'em distraught. What's worse, your grandfather, Peter, is after marryin' your gram, Kathleen, and such evil luck is a bad omen for their upcomin' nuptials.

"Well, Meghan and John call in a priest and an old hedge witch in the neighborhood too (on the sly for the priest is disapprovin' of the old folk ways). The priest blesses the house and walks around deosil with holy water and a censer of incense. Next day come the old gal, walkin' widdershins with burnin' sage and herbs.

"Well, the hedge witch stops stock-still at Maggie's bedroom window and starts screamin' and carryin' on about the source of the evil and their daughter bein' a witch for true. After rantin' and ravin' in the road outside the cottage, she runs off through the fields, nearly lightin' them on fire with her smudge pot as she goes.

"Your great grandmother sets her mind to get to the bottom of things, still in shock at her eldest daughter's sudden departure a few years past. Rumor and a few postcards of St. Patrick's Cathedral of Ireland have given her the knowledge that Maggie is somewhere in Dublin, so Meghan takes it upon herself to travel there to hunt Maggie down.

"Poor Meghan, the city is a bit much for her and, not havin' folks there, she goes to Saint Patrick's to inquire of rooms fit for a good Catholic woman searchin' for her long lost child. Well, as destiny would have it, your great grandmother didn't have long to stay for, roundin' the corner of the street the good priest sends her to, she spies a bright, brick-faced shop on the other side of the road and, hungry and tired to her bones, she ducks in for tea and a biscuit.

"It's already late in the day and the shop is empty of customers. The girl in the back is busyin' herself cleanin' up and puttin' cakes away when Meghan pops in.

"'Is it too late for some tea?', she asks meekly, not wantin' to be a bother when the shop's clearly closin'.

"The shop girl turns to face her, and your great grandmother sits down right there grabbin' a good hold on the table edge, for there is her own Maggie. But a Maggie only a mother would recognize for, if your great grandmother didn't know better, she'd have thought her own little

48

teenaged Molly had followed her to Dublin, so young and so pretty was the girl before her. At first Meghan doubted her eyes and took it to be the effects of a sleepless night on the train. But then she got a good look at the beauty before her and saw the mark on her lip.

"'God's kiss!' she gasped, and all doubt was erased from her mind when a great look of shock crossed the girl's face, so surprised was she to turn and see her own mother standin' there in her shop that the teapot she was holdin' fell from her hand and crashed to the ground in a million smithers.

"Meghan could do nothing more than sit there with her hand clapped over her mouth as her daughter raced around the counter and took hold of her, cryin'.

"Now, these days, a young woman could claim she'd won the lottery and spent it all on plastic surgery but, so great was Maggie's transformation that, even that story, were it in fashion, would have had the listener doubtin' the truth of it. She had gone from a beast to an angel.

"Yer great aunt put up the "Closed" sign in the front door and began to race around the room, makin' tea and puttin' out all sorts of dainties for her mother. It seemed as if her luck had changed as entirely as her looks. She was happy as a lark and had friends aplenty to talk of, what with meetin' so many what came to her shop for conversation. She chattered on and on as Meghan sat there weak and worried in spite of her daughter's good fortune because she could no more believe that it wasn't ill gotten than she could believe the sun switched places with the moon. After some time, Maggie settled down, sat beside her mum, took her trembling hand and finally thought to ask after the family she'd left behind.

"O' course, Meghan had naught but sad tales to tell of Aidan's poor dead children and all the sorrow that had come upon them. Great Aunt Maggie reacted with a strange discomfort. The magpie grew quiet and tried to change the course of the conversation with a simple, solemn shake of her head. 'Too bad, it is,' she said, and got up to about her business finishin' with the cleanin'.

"'Yeh must stay with me awhile, mother, for I have a nice little flat right here above the shop and 'tis fine and comfy with more cakes and sandwiches at hand!'

"'Maggie, I come to find yeh and to make what I can of the goings on at home. Sissy, the old hedge witch, come to the house just last week, kickin' up a fuss over yeh. She's blamin' our ill fortune on yeh, callin' yeh a witch.'

"Maggie wheeled around, angry as a wet bee. 'And you'd be after believin' her mother?'

"'What can I make of this, child? Look at yeh! Even if your features were the same, there'd still be the matter of yer havin' found the fountain of youth! Yer a woman of thirty-two, I what gave birth to yeh should know, and yeh look almost as young as your baby sister!'

"The girl knew there was little sense in arguin' against plain fact but now a fear came upon her. The banshee's curse hadn't seemed real to her before this. When she was putterin' around her shop, busy and happy, she'd thought little of the fate of those she'd left behind. It was a choice she'd made and, every day when she looked in the mirror at her unfadin' beauty, she told herself it was the right choice, nay, the only one. Maggie broke down and told her mother the whole story and pleaded for her understandin'.

"'I meant no one any harm, mother. When the banshee laid the curse it was already too late. I've sorrowed over it and hoped that the worst would not come to pass, that the banshee wouldn't have the power. But mother, as you can see, if the banshee's curse could not be lifted, then stayin' would've only made matters worse. Would you be wantin' me to stay locked up all me life, mother? Or to have folks see me this way and have the whole family accused of harborin' a witch?!'

"So it was that Meghan went home with a heavy heart. She told the family everything. Your grandfather, Peter, was perhaps the most upset of all. Aidan's sorrows were explained but, bad as it was, he had two lovely girls left to dote on. Peter was set on marryin' your gram, Kathleen, but how could he do this when his vow to her would be a promise of sorrow to come?"

"Dad," Brian said, "if everybody believed all this crap about the curse and Uncle Aidan and his wife had lost their two boys, how did this other Connor boy.... "

"Yeah," threw in Sean, "this is a really cool story but I've got a lot to do. Can you get to the part about our dead cousin?"

"Alright, I'm getting to that," Dad replied, dropping his accent and taking a good long drink of tea. He drained the cup and paused a bit after, miffed to have anyone interrupt his dramatic finish. Finally, he cleared his throat.

"Ahem! To shorten it a bit for those of you who have more important things to think of than your heritage...like Halo," he eyed Sean. "...Grandfather Peter and Grandmother Kathleen determined to leave for America, hoping the curse would not come to foreign soil. And, since I have five younger brothers with children of their own, it seems like it worked just fine. Back in Ireland, great-uncle, Aidan, and his wife bore no more children for a long time. Then, twenty-one years ago, when the both of them thought their child rearing days behind them and your great-aunt Maureen was almost embarrassed to have a baby, a summer night found them a wee bit frisky and a great bit careless, and your cousin, Aidan Jr., was born the next spring. He thought he'd escaped the curse and was here to celebrate and, maybe, to assure his continued fortune by spending his twenty-first year in the states. But it looks like he couldn't escape the Irish Connor fate."

Saturday night's events raced through my mind and my chicken thigh threatened to come back up for a visit as I finally realized where the second banshee at the club had come from. She'd followed one of the Irish Connors here, and that could mean nothing good for any of us.

*

Personally, I think anyone who *wants* to be in touch with the supernatural is bat shit crazy. I mean, there's all these cable shows about these loony people going into haunted shops and houses and digging around in attics for ghosts and having séances and crap. Why? Maybe my imagination is too vivid but, Dad's stories always weirded me out. My brothers would go to bed after one of Dad's folktales about witches or fairies on the heath, saying how cool it was. Me? I like risk and daring as much as the next person, but I prefer my fear factor to be raised by roller coasters at Six Flags or the rush of getting up to sing in front of a couple of hundred people. I was never a fan of creatures that steal babies or drag you off to fairy land in an eternal stupor.

After Dad's story was over, I went to get ready for bed. The good thing about having the only bedroom on the bottom floor is having the downstairs bathroom all to myself at night. I sopped off my makeup with baby oil and brushed my teeth. The white, foamy toothpaste made me think of a rabid banshee. Everything was making me think of banshees.

I was only borderline comfortable with the O'Donnell banshee, and that only because she'd shared my grief. Old red-eye was another thing entirely. Still, I didn't want to see either of them again and now I had to return to the room where, just that afternoon, the pale messenger had visited for the second time. Her words had frightened me and, now that I understood the curse, they frightened me even more.

"And more will perish," she had said. I knew what that meant. Other Connor boys were going to die. And Dad, being the oldest in his family, well....that meant his boys were first in line. Probably even Dad himself or my uncles who had all managed to cheat the curse thus far. What had Maggie's banshee said? "....any male child born to yer father's line will be cut down before he takes a breath past his twenty-first year." Michael and Patrick were already twenty-one. Their birthday was coming up in the spring. All my brothers had already lived longer than any of Uncle Aidan's heirs except Aidan Jr. Poor Uncle Aidan.

The toothpaste foam suddenly made me gag so I spat and rinsed. I checked the time on my cell phone. 10:26 p.m. I'd set the TV timer in my room for ten p.m. so it would bring in noise and light and chase the banshee away. I hoped.

I walked down the hall cautiously and tapped the door open wide before I dared to step in. No sign of her. Evidently the banshee wasn't a fan of Cartoon Network.

*

Farrell was back in school in about a week and a half, and one of the first things he did was stick a note on my locker.

"Meet me at the diner after school. My treat."

Hmmm. Farrell was trying to be nice to me. Had they made a mistake in the hospital and performed a lobotomy instead of an appendectomy? Or was Los's call about the lawsuit dead on? Would he be waiting for me in the diner with some guy in a pin stripe suit and a legal pad? I can't say my curiosity was piqued so much as my sense of guilt. I still felt badly about smashing his hand and my brothers throwing him over the fence when he was only trying to help me.

When I got to the diner, Farrell was alone. He ordered a large coke for me almost before I sat down and handed me the *War and Peace*-sized menu.

"Get anything you want. Dinner even."

I looked at him suspiciously.

"Don't say it if you don't mean it. Dad's working late and Dylan is making his famous cardboard-pizza-from-frozen-food-hell."

"Nah, Brandy. I mean it. Go ahead. The works. Anything you want. I owe you an apology."

I dropped the menu on the table, crossed my arms and looked at him askance.

"What's up, Farr? What do you mean, you owe *me* an apology? I'm the one that slammed the window on your hand. By accident!" I added quickly in case he was taping the conversation for insurance or something.

Farrell leaned over the table and looked at me. Those eyes. I couldn't recall which had done me in more when I'd first met him, those lips or those melty brown eyes.

I looked down, afraid I was blushing like some idiot. Idiot or not, I still had feelings for Farrell, I had to admit. If dad hadn't caught us that afternoon, he might still be my boyfriend. But my grounding had pointed out the issues involved with having a girlfriend lead singer and, with Farrell, the band came first. Combined with the fact that I had made the huge mistake of telling him about The Lady and he already thought I was certifiably crazy, he'd broken up

55

with me. After that, it was strictly business. We got on each other's nerves but, sometimes, I figured that was because of our history. And sometimes I still felt a little spark between us.

"That's okay. If you want to, you can say we're even. You owed me one, Bran. I was...I was really nasty to you when we broke up."

"We? YOU broke up with *me*."

"Yeah, well...I can see now that at least some of my reasons were..."

"Unfounded?" I offered.

"I was going to say lame but, yeah, if unfounded means a bad reason then, yeah."

"You told me I was fubar and teased me about fairies. Ouch!" I flashed a little smile, not wanting to sound accusatory and spoil things. After all, I probably wouldn't have believed me either.

"I know, I know. And I'm really sorry. I really thought you were two cards short of a deck until," he lowered his eyes and twisted the paper cover from his drinking straw over in a tight knot between his fingers, "...before... before your cousin died like that."

"Pretty freaky, huh?"

"Yeah. After I found out who the guy was and put all the pieces together I felt like a real jerk for yanking your chain all the time about leprechauns and house brownies."

"And unicorns."

"Yeah." Farrell really seemed chagrined. I might have told him so if I'd thought he had the slightest idea what the word meant. He looked down at his hands again. I looked too. The bruise I'd created was pretty much a faded memory.

"I saw all that glass breaking and all that wind blowing around. And the feedback. That wasn't....it wasn't feedback, was it, Bran?"

"No. Feedback doesn't kill people."

Farrell almost knocked over his drink.

"Kill people? Wait a minute. You told me that banshees *announce* deaths, not cause them."

"Yeah, well, normally, that's true. They do. They announce the deaths of the members of families they're attached to. But this banshee might be different."

The waitress came. I ordered and slowly went through a huge plate of disco fries as I relayed Dad's story about Great Aunt Maggie and the Connor curse. It took a second order of fries to finish the tale.

"Whoa!" Farrell, whose mouth had been hanging open for pretty much the entire story, used it to say something at last. "That's some heavy shit! Do you think it's true?"

I shrugged.

"Well, is everyone okay? Anybody sick or anything?"

"Everyone's fine...so far. I mean, it's only been two weeks but, so far, all the US Connors are okay. We haven't heard any bad news or anything from our cousins in Jersey City and my brothers are all well, but..."

"But what?"

"But...nothing." Things were going nice with us. Farrell was being sweet and he had listened - really listened - to my story. I didn't want to spoil things.

"Don't do that, Bran. Now you've got my

imagination going!"

I took a deep breath and blew it out forcefully. "You're going to say I'm nuts again."

Farrell reached across the table and took my hand.

"Brandy, the night that crap went down at the club I was scared out of my mind. But, as scared as I was of what was going on around me, my first thought was about you. I...I still care about you, Bran. And after all that shit, I'm not going to think you're nuts even if you tell me that you went home last night and found a pixie dancing in your pajamas."

I laughed at the image. Oh, what the hell, I thought. We're already broken up. I couldn't make it worse. No harm, no foul.

"Well," I said finally, "next week is Halloween."

"Ooh! The night the dead rise from their graves."

There didn't seem to be any sarcasm intended.

"Yeah. The Celts called it Samhain. The night the dead revisit the mortal world. In Ireland there are some who say the dead rise up and dance on the heaths."

"Lucky they don't have heaths in Dover, New Jersey, huh?" Farrell interjected. I frowned. "They don't, do they?" I frowned even more. "Sorry. Just joking, Bran. Not making fun of you or anything, honest."

I shook my head, rolled my eyes, and continued.

"The Irish have lots of traditions for Halloween. My mum always made colcannon on that night. It's just some smashed up potatoes and kale. She'd wrap coins in brown paper and stuff them inside the bowl for us kids to find and keep. Then, after supper, we'd all have a slice of Bambrack Cake. It's a kind of fruit bread that gets baked with a coin, a piece of rag, and a ring inside. We'd all watch each other to see who got what. The coin means you'll have a prosperous year, the rag means you'll have to watch your money, and the ring means happiness or even romance is headed your way."

I stopped, hoping Farrell had forgotten the original question. He hadn't.

"Bran, none of that sounds spooky. Why are you so worried about Halloween?"

I picked up a piece of potato and sopped up all the remaining cheese and gravy. The last disco fry slid down my throat in a lump.

"The last thing we do is this ivy leaf thing. You know all that ivy growing over by the front gate by my house?"

"Yeah, I fell in that after I rolled out of the friggin' hedges," he said with a benign little smirk that made him look cute.

"On Halloween night every member of the family takes one fresh ivy leaf and puts it inside a cup of water before they go to bed. In the morning, if the leaf is still perfect and hasn't got any spots on it, then that person will have a year of health. If not...."

My voice trailed. Unexpected and unwelcome tears started to well up in my eyes. Crap! Despite the hospital fainting scene, it was not like me to get emotional. Farrell reached over and grabbed my greasy fingers.

"Don't worry, Bran. Don't worry. I'll be there for you this time. No matter what."

"Don't say it if you don't mean it. I might need your help."

"No matter what. I swear," he replied, licking a last bit of gravy off my pinky and sending almost as many chills down my spine as the banshees.

*

Halloween became less fun for me once I got too old to go out in costume. I tried to fill my cos-lust by dressing weird at school sometimes but it wasn't the same. As the lead singer in a band, wearing funky clothes was almost the law. The school's "no costume" policy (decreed lest gang members sneak into the school disguised as nuns or something) only made matters worse. I was nervous all day on Halloween and there was nothing exciting to take my mind off of things. Even the kid who had gotten kicked out of school two years in a row for coming to class dressed in drag decided to obey the "no costume" dictum. I drudged through my classes distractedly, eating candy corn surreptitiously under my desk when possible. It was a good day to goof off since the teachers were chalking up all distracted behavior to sugar rushes. To cheer myself up a little when I got home, I stuck on a lame witch's hat just to get in the spirit for the trick or treaters, then I ran to the kitchen to start the potatoes for the colcannon.

Dinner was very late because - good as I was in the kitchen - Bambrack cake was definitely not in my repertoire. Dad had to detour to Gram's after work and pick up one of hers. The family, some steaks, and the colcannon were waiting for him when he arrived and we were all so starved that the mash was devoured in record time with every coin discovered before the last morsel was doled out. Still, as much as we'd eaten, we were all eager for cake.

"Bet I get the ring this year!" said Michael. "I'm feeling lucky about that new girl at work!"

"Is she a hottie?" asked Sean.

"That'll be enough," replied Dad stiffly. 'Whoa! What's this?" He slowly pulled out a long strip of white rag from his mouthful. Poverty. Loss. I felt awful. Dad needed a break. Even though it was all in fun, I wanted him to get one of the good items. As it turned out, I got the ring. My recently resurrected romance with Farrell might have explained that well enough but I didn't share that thought.

The coin that symbolized wealth and prosperity was the last item. And nowhere to be found. Though we all chewed our soft cake well enough, no one's tooth hit metal and, when we'd all had seconds and Patrick had taken to shredding the remaining heel of fruit bread between his fingers, there was still no coin.

"Gram is slipping," observed Patrick.

"I don't think so," corrected Dad. "She's got this down to a science. I think one of you gluttons swallowed it. My money's on a treasure in the toilet tomorrow." He wiped his mouth and rose from the table. "I'm going out for the ivy. Get your cups ready."

I got up and went to the cabinet next to the

sink and, as my brothers filed past with their now empty supper dishes, I handed a glass to each of them in turn. By the time the table was cleared and the dishwasher loaded, Dad had returned with a small branch of ivy.

"Did you shake if off real good at the door?" I asked, trying to sound nonchalant.

"No spiders, my love," answered Dad, guessing my concern. Yes, another one of tough Brandy Connor's weaknesses. So? Big macho Indiana Jones hates snakes, and I also knew that my huge lug of a brother, Sean, the linebacker, was even more afraid of spiders than I was, although he would never admit it.

Dad scrutinized the branch and hand-picked the foliage slowly, careful to choose only the most pristine specimens. As we filed past, he held a tiny leaf over each of our glasses and said, "God bless!" as he dropped it in. I thought it was sort of like a green, pagan communion but, as I held my own glass out to him, I didn't dare make that analogy out loud.

"Mmmmm...kiss kiss, Dad," I said, pecking him on his forehead. His hairline was receding and there was more gray in what was left than I'd remembered. Mom's death had been so hard on him. Another reason why I was hoping this year's ivy tradition would turn out perfectly.

When we were all finished, Sean left for a party dressed as the Incredible Hulk. He didn't need much of a costume. Patrick and Brian opted for television while Michael and Dylan went to their rooms for "homework" aka Facebook. Dad was in his favorite chair reading the paper and waiting for the late news when I went to my room to read some old Neil Gaiman comics. I loved The Sandman and, tired as I was, I was counting on Morpheus and the gang to hold my interest until midnight at least. If either of the banshees were going to start acting up, midnight on Halloween seemed like the most likely time and I wanted to be alert and ready. Or at least awake.

I was lost in Season of Mists when I glanced at the clock. 12:08. The witching hour had passed. A huge sigh came spilling out of me. I hadn't even realized that I was holding my breath. Adjusting my stiff shoulders into a more comfortable position, I continued to read until my eyes closed and my brothers' loud TV show faded from my consciousness.

I'd scarcely been asleep when I heard shouting from the upstairs bedroom.

"What the hell?"

SLAM! Heavy footsteps. CRASH!

"Son of a bitch! Which one of you assholes did this?"

The digital alarm read 1:13 a.m. I leapt to my feet and ran to the front of the darkened house and up the stairs to find Sean, still covered in Hulky-green body paint, standing in the middle of the hallway, eyeing the glass shards and water strewn all around his bare feet.

"Who the hell did this?"

Dad's conservation campaign meant that the hall was lit with a 40 watt bulb, but from the landing I could see the water seeping outward from the broken glass in a slow circle. I took two steps closer and stopped dead, realizing with a little choke of terror that it wasn't water at all. The dim light from the old fixture fell on dozens of tiny, transparent spiders rippling in waves from a small dark central object - a decrepit and decayed looking ivy leaf.

Patrick and Michael's door opened first on the left.

"What the hell's all the commotion about? We've got work in the morning. What the...?" Patrick took a step back inside the door jamb as he realized that an endless army of spiders was moving towards his feet. Dad popped out next and took a proactive approach, ducking back in his room for his slippers and returning in a flash to begin smashing the spiders with them at arm's length.

"What the hell is going ON out there?" shouted Michael from his bed.

As Dad slapped at the creatures red-faced, he glanced up at Sean's terrified expression and Patrick's mouth-breathing stare.

"Well, don't just stand there! Someone go get the Raid!"

From where the hideous mess lay seething ever outward, Dylan's room was the only clear path to the bathroom at the end of the hall.

"Dylan!" screamed Sean, frozen by the fear of cutting his feet as well as of the relentless, crawling mass, now inches from his toes on the landing.

"Sssssssssss! Don't wake your brother!" shushed Dad.

But it was too late. Dylan's door creaked open. He was up already, going to get a drink of water I supposed from the glass in his hand. Then I took a look at his face. It was white as snow on a grave.

No one noticed him but me. Sean was already moving gingerly backwards towards his doorway, hoping for the squirming flood to abate. Patrick had followed Dad's lead and had disappeared into his room momentarily, emerging in seconds sporting his untied work boots to join in stomping on the nightmarish swarm flowing from down the sides of the glass like a Niagara of arachnids. Only I noticed Dylan's expression. He glanced at the battle raging against the spiders, then down at his glass, and then back up through the commotion to meet my eyes where I was standing at the top of the landing.

"Bran?" he said weakly.

Some courage took hold of me and I went running straight through the spiders, the stomping, and the shards. A piece of glass stabbed my foot and I winced but managed to hobble for the last few steps. I grabbed the glass from Dylan's hand. In the dim light at the end of the hall I looked down and gasped at the sight of a single, shriveled ivy leaf afloat in a thick, blood red liquid.

Chapter 4 – Brotherly Love

"So maybe Patrick or Michael were screwin' around with everyone's head and..."

"Seriously, Farrell, Patrick woke up the next day and his leaf was covered with a slimy white fungus that smelled like the devil's underwear. And Michael's was full of holes and crawling with these tiny maggoty looking things that looked like no bug I've ever seen in years of Discovery Channel viewing so, that would be a no."

I watched Farrell open his mouth to speak.

"Brian ran to throw his in the john after the spider/blood thing, and as far as my dad having anything to do with it, don't even go there."

He clicked his jaw shut and stirred his coffee for the ninth time since I'd begun telling him the full story of the Halloween horror-fest at the Connors. We were at the diner again, meeting for a few secret alone minutes after rehearsal. Since Dad didn't like Farrell in the first place, and had too much on his mind in the second place, I had decided against breaking the news of our reconciliation to him until... I had no game plan for "until". Maybe Farrell and I'd break up again anyway. It was a possibility. Especially since I was planning on asking Farrell for a favor that might blow our entire relationship out of the water.

"What about the banshees? Have you seen either of them?"

"How could I? I was in the emergency

room until almost 5 a.m. getting stitches in my foot. It amazes me how many people can manage to get hurt after midnight! Anyway, banshees don't come out in the day time, so no on that too. I slept all day yesterday. If they'd both showed up and had a party I wouldn't have noticed because I was trashed on the pain killers the doctor gave me."

Farrell sunk back into his seat in the booth. He combed his shaggy brown hair from his eyes with his fingers and tapped his spoon on the table. I was making him fidgety. Now that he believed my banshee stories it was sort of worse. Before he could lighten the tension by teasing me about being a lunatic, now it was real and, therefore, really frightening. Farrell probably felt like he was dating Sookie Stackhouse.

"Wow, Bran. That...sucks." He avoided my eyes, looking down at the spoon he was now rolling over in his fingers. "So, what are you going to do?"

What was *I* going to do? Where was "I'll be there for you this time"? I assessed his uneasy expression. Would his resolve to help me weaken in direct proportion to his fear? I was about to ask a favor that was tantamount to asking a paraplegic to give you his wheelchair, but Farrell's expression made me wonder if I could count on him for picking up the tab for coffee.

I took a deep breath to curb my emotions. If he reneged on his pre-make-up promise of ends-of-the-earth support and I lost my temper, the whole thing would be blown, not to mention that I wasn't going to storm out of the diner very easily with three new stitches in my foot from the glass shard.

"Well, I've been giving this a lot of thought," I said calmly. "I figure, the only way to stop this thing is to find Maggie."

"What for? How the hell are you going to do that?" His incredulous tone told me immediately that my idea was going to be a hard sell.

"Well, to answer your first question, my great aunt is the one who caused this whole thing, so it only makes sense to me that she's the one who can stop it."

"Brandy, your Dad said the banshee didn't want the comb back..."

"That's right, she doesn't. But what she does want is freedom...."

Farrell interrupted. "So what are you going to do? Form some sort of banshee liberation front?"

I poked my fork into a piece of the Death by Chocolate layer cake we were sharing and stuck it squarely into Farrell's mouth.

"Shut up and listen for just a minute," I said impatiently. Then, remembering the task ahead and catching myself, I smiled again and said "Please?" so nauseatingly sweetly that I almost up-chucked the burger I'd just eaten.

Farrell nodded and chewed the sticky mouthful, muttering assent.

"I've been doing a lot of reading on Irish folklore. One story I read said that a banshee's soul could be freed if she finds someone willing to take her place." Farrell opened his mouth again but I plowed on. "Maggie is almost 80 years old. Maybe if I go to see her, tell her what the curse has done to her family, maybe by now she'll be ready to do the right thing and end it."

Farrell let out a sarcastic little laugh.

"Brandy, if you were eighty and still looked like a hottie would you want to give that up? She might even be immortal. And she probably doesn't even remember her own family much less care about a bunch of American relatives that she has never met."

I could feel my lips pursing into a just-sucked-a-lemon position. I knew he was right. I had come up with the same objections in my own head every minute since I'd gotten the idea but I knew that I had to ignore the logic of it or go crazy waiting in helpless immobility while my family was threatened. I bit the inside of my cheek and struggled to keep my tone even.

"I know, you're probably right, Farrell, but if it were your family, wouldn't you want to try everything and anything you could to help?" I laid one of my hands around his and lifted the other to wipe a small stray bit of frosting off his chin, parting his lips gently with my finger to let him lick it off. I closed my eyes as if the wet warmth of his tongue was lifting me to new heights of passion, but I was mentally calculating my next step. I flashed a three-packages-of-aspartame smile his way and hated myself for it.

"Farr, remember when you said you'd be there for me if anything happened." He gave me that deer-caught-in-the-headlights look. "You said, 'No matter what'...."

"I said that?" He stared at me with one eyebrow cocked and a smirk that said he was thinking of a wise crack. As I witnessed his pre-reconciliation "my hero" resolve melting away, my blood immediately started to simmer. Rapidly losing confidence in the direct approach, I plodded on, knowing I had a backup plan.

"It's not such a big thing, really. I just need a little loan."

Farrell worked for his Dad on the weekends, laying in wood flooring, and he got paid the going foreign-day-laborer rate of one hundred dollars a day. It was hard work and Farrell had once balked and demanded more. That day his Dad had driven the pickup to Blackwell Street at six a.m. and actually picked up a foreign day laborer, which caused Farrell to suddenly realize the benefits of working with his Dad over minimum wage at Burger King - no hours that cut into band practice and no risk of an acne condition induced by hanging around the fryers. Even though he liked to blow money on eating out and shopping trips to Dark Towers and GameStop, I knew he had a good chunk stashed in his room.

Farr nodded dumbly, still staring at the coffee and cream ripples he was making with his spoon.

"I told you I'd be there for you, Bran, and I meant it. I can loan you a couple of bucks. How much do you need?" He was back in "my hero" mode.

"Oh! I knew I could count on you!" I said in my best Drama III ingénue voice, purposely overplaying. "I just need about six hundred dollars."

"SIX HUNDRED BUCKS?!"

Farrell shouted it so loudly that every head

in the diner turned to look at us. I stared them all back down. What? It wasn't like he shouted out "penis" or something.

"Farr," I jumped in before he could continue with the expected negative. It was clear that the anticipated result of my directness – Farrell immediately and cheerfully agrees to loan me the money – was going to be a wash. I put Plan B into immediate effect, leaning across the table and cupping his hands under mine around the warm coffee mug. It was time to act positive, lay it on thick, and clinch the deal with a fake offer he couldn't refuse.

"I want you to know that your doing this means a whole hell of a lot to me, Farr. It makes me feel...so much closer to you." I lowered my voice and gave him my most nauseating cow-eyed stare. "I know you've wanted to take things to the next step and, after you loan me this money, I intend to show you all my love and gratitude."

My ace was on the table. As were my boobs. I took a deep breath and smiled as he cocked his head like a puppy hearing the word "walk" or "cookie", all puzzled and anticipatory. He looked at me deeply. Then he moved his eyes from my cleavage to my expectant face and his smile faded. I watched as he nodded dumbly. In the negative.

"Don't you want me?" I pushed out my lower lip in a pout, trying to look completely boo-boo faced. God! I was disgusting myself.

"I...I'm really sorry, Bran. It's not that. You know I want you. But...but I can't give you the money. You know I'm saving for a new guitar. And you know I've had to squirrel away the cash

71

bit by bit cuz my dad checks my bank statements. He'd never let me buy another guitar. I've been saving so long and I'm almost halfway to my goal. I could spare a hundred maybe but...six hundred bucks would set me back a long time! And even if you could pay me back, it would take you ages."

Farrell had rejected my best offer. Mentally, my jaw dropped. Mentally, I was indignant. Mentally, I was leaping across the table and pounding him with the metal napkin holder. But, with both Plan A and B a wash, I had to keep my cool even more. If Farrell was pissing me off it was a good thing. I needed to hold onto that pissed off feeling to put Plan C into action.

*

If I'd had the slightest qualm about what I was going to do, the slightest doubt about the necessity to do it, it disappeared on the 12th of November.

As the days shortened, White Noise began to schedule rehearsals earlier. This made Stan's mom happy because she had complained all summer that she hated the noise when she was watching TV late at night, and it made me happy cuz I could get home at a decent enough hour to claim "library" as an excuse and avoid another "discussion" with my dad about how I was defying him and wasting my time with White Noise. I was trying very hard not to upset Dad. I ran home after school on the 12th, checked on the stew in the crock pot, grabbed a tote with my music stuff in it, and made my way the two blocks to Stan's in my new Converse kicks with skulls on them.

I took the painted grey steps to the porch two at a time, bounced through the open front door, and flew down to the basement. The guys were still setting up and there were wire cases and crap all over the floor. I opened my mike case, set it in the stand and still had time to haul myself up onto Stan's mom's washing machine for a minute.

Braaaaaaappppppppppppp. The cell phone in my back pocket reverberated against the metal lid like a single engine prop. I wiggled off and fished it out. It was Michael.

"Bran?"

"Yeah, Mike, what's up? I checked the crock pot if that's what you're worried about. You coming home late?"

"Umm...well, yeah. I'm at St. Clare's."

"Oh, cripe! What's wrong?"

"Well, basically, it's Sean."

"Sean? Basically? What happened? What are you talking about?"

"Bran. You'd better go home and hold down the fort. Sean had an accident at football practice. I'm going to be here awhile..."

"I'm coming down, Mike!"

"No! Don't! There's too much commotion here and Dad's on his way. Just go home and check on dinner and put the lights on for us and sit tight. And call me if you hear from Dylan. I can't get in touch with him."

"He's out in the field with band practice. His cell's probably off. I'll wait for him home. Did you call Brian and Patrick."

"Well, um, yeah. I did. But...well...that's another thing."

"What?"

"Patrick got into a little accident on his way over here. I'm sure he's okay. He called me from Route 46. He's on his way now in an ambulance."

I felt dizzy and lightheaded. I was beginning to learn that my "toughness" was more about a bad temper than it was about avoiding fainting or puking in a crisis, but I pulled myself together.

"Oh my god, Mike. You keep calling me, okay? You let me know everything and anything as soon as you hear!"

I clicked my crappy refurbished clamshell phone shut.

"Hey, guys....I have an emergency."

Collective moan.

"Cut the crap! My brothers are in the hospital for Christ's sake!"

Silence.

"ALL of them?" said Farrell, dumbstruck.

"No, Sean and Patrick. I don't have time to explain. If you care, text me later when I'll know more."

I ran out. I had to get home to wait for Dylan and stop the crock pot from burning the house down.

*

I'd like to be able to say that I breathed a sigh of relief when Dylan walked in the door at six p.m. but I had the job of telling him why no one else was home. Worse yet, when I told him he started to cry.

"This is that banshee thing, isn't it? From

the blood and all the spiders and shit at Halloween!"

"It's just a stroke of bad luck," I fibbed in the most soothing voice possible. "Coincidences. Bad, bad coincidences. I'm sure they'll both be just fine."

He walked off into the living room and sat in the Laz-E-Boy just staring at the blank TV screen.

Around a quarter to seven, Michael called and told us that Brian was at St. Clare's and to start supper without them. I called a reluctant Dylan to the table and ladled out microscopic portions of stew because I knew neither of us would eat it. We waited there in silence, picking at a pea here, a carrot slice there, for nearly an hour. Around eight, Dad called and asked me to get some clothes together for him so he could spend the night with Sean. Brian came for them around nine.

"Go to bed, Bran. No use the whole family staying up. It's...it's gonna be alright."

He had the same voice I'd used on Dylan and I wasn't buying it, but I didn't say so.

I gave him a hug as I handed him the overnight bag with Dad's things in it.

"Yes, I'm sure they will be. I'll light a candle for them in my room."

I honestly don't know how I fell asleep. I had gone to my room to read because Dylan had finally gone up and locked himself in his, disconsolate. He screamed at me when I'd knocked at his door and tried to comfort him.

"I have some Swiss Miss for you, D! The double chocolate kind. Your favorite."

"Go AWAY, Bran! I don't want anything right now! Just LEAVE ME ALONE!"

So I'd drunk the cocoa myself. Maybe that was it. Sleep-inducing carbs? At any rate, I nodded off sometime after ten with a candle burning on my dresser in front of mom's funeral parlor prayer card of the Virgin Mary. Not that I really thought it could help but, it couldn't hurt, right?

It was midnight when I woke up shivering. The candle was out. It had been the tall, elegant, dinner kind, set in a holder on a dish and, even in the darkness, I could make out its white form and see that it hadn't burned all the way down.

Caoine. That's the Irish word for the cry of mourners. The sound of the banshee that had once been described in a book I was reading as a keening that rose to a sob that moved to a wail and finally climbed to a screeching that sounded like the tortured souls of the damned. Why the hell did I read so damn much?

Right now all I heard was soft, low moaning. Dylan? He'd have to be moaning pretty fiercely for me to hear him downstairs. Was anyone else home? If I never heard Dad or any of my older brothers cry aloud after Mom died, I didn't think it would make sense for me to hear it now.

What if something awful happened to Sean or Patrick?

I gasped at the thought and sat bolt upright, fully awake, immediately catching a glimpse of the source of the sounds. The pretty O'Donnell banshee was back in my window, combing her hair and sniffling, wiping her spectral eyes on a gossamer sleeve that I could see through to the yard outside my window. My heart began to pound so loudly that I thought she'd hear it and disperse from the sound of its drumming.

In the yard I saw the wild, red-eyed Irish banshee tearing around in flight through the air, laughing and shrieking. Her milky figure streaked over the bushes and through the knobby, arthritic branches of the old apple tree that stood black against the dim sky, twisting its gnarled joints upwards tensely, as if supplicating mercy from an unhearing god.

"So it begins," cried The Lady, pulling out another thick strand of white hair. It disintegrated like melting cotton candy as it streamed towards the floor.

I didn't have to ask her what she was talking about.

*

I nodded off in class so many times the next day at school that my art teacher, Miss Carrozza, threatened to send me to the clinic for a drug test. Finally, she called me out into the hall and, when I told her what had happened at home, she wrote a note to the school nurse and I got to nap in her office for the last two periods.

Michael picked me up at the gate after school.

"Crap, Mike," I said as I sank into the bucket seats of his Ford. "I don't' know why Dad wouldn't let me come to the hospital today. I was so worried. School was a total waste."

"Bran, there was nothing you could do there and Dad's pretty upset. I don't think he wanted you to see him until he pulled himself together."

"Is he doing better now? How are Patrick and Sean?"

Mike shrugged. "Well, Patrick looks terrible but he's not so bad off. They had to use the jaws-of-life to pull him out of his car. He had a broken clavicle, a broken arm, and a foot fractured in five places. Add to that assorted cuts and bruises and, well, he threw a scare into me when I saw him but don't worry, his condition is....good." His words sounded strained.

"You're lying, Michael. I always know when you're lying."

I turned away and stared at the side of the road a moment. I felt as cold and lost as the wind-tossed leaves stirring up in the gutters.

"And Sean?" I looked back at Mike. He was staring straight ahead, glassy-eyed, so I dropped it when he didn't answer and we rode the rest of the way in silence.

When the automatic doors to the hospital lobby slid open, I could see Dad sitting in the nubby brown chairs in the waiting area. I sat next to him while Mike went up to the desk for the visitor cards.

Dad proceeded to try to "prepare me" for the sight of my brothers' injuries by telling me it all looked worse than it was. It didn't help.

As for my unanswered question about Sean? Well, his condition, it turned out, was impossible to sugar coat. He was in a coma with a head injury and there was really no telling when or even if he was going to come out of it. I steeled myself as the olive green elevator doors closed in front of the three of us and the lift rose to the intensive care unit.

My heart was beating in my throat as we made our way to Patrick's room through the halls with their smells of dying flowers and disinfectant. Patrick was asleep and it was just as well because I wouldn't have wanted him to hear the gasp that flew from my mouth when I saw him. Nothing Dad or Mike had said had prepared me for this. He was a mess. There wasn't a spot on him that wasn't the livid red of a fresh bruise or a cold, bloodless blue white. I went to touch his hand but it had an IV needle stuck in it and the creeping yellow edge of another bruise seeped out from the tape that held it in place. Two hot tears rolled out of my eyes and dropped onto the edge of his waffle blanket but I bit my lip and held in the rest.

After awhile we walked soberly to Sean's room. I was ready for a real visual nightmare but, surprisingly, Sean looked for all the world like nothing at all had happened to him. Aside from his chalky white skin, three thousand feet of clear polyvinyl tubing sticking out all over, and a respirator machine that sounded like Darth Vader was in the room with us, he looked like a sleeping angel. There wasn't a visible scratch on him.

"The doctors don't know what's wrong," Dad offered suddenly.

"Huh? I thought...I thought he was in a coma."

"Oh, yes, he's in a coma. And he's having trouble breathing. But the doctors don't know why."

"But...I don't understand. Didn't you say he had a head injury in football practice?"

"Yes, he did, but all the x-rays and CAT scans and the MRI don't show anything more than a mild concussion. According to the doctor, he should be up and around, talking with us."

"Well, why don't you get a specialist in to see him?"

"That *was* the report of the specialist."

I stared at Sean's face, close to the color of the snowy hospital linens. The respirator clicked and wheezed, clicked and wheezed. The clear IV fluid dripped down like a maniac's idea of a time machine, ticking away the remnants of my brother's health as his strong body lay useless and immobile. If the banshee's modus operandi was "wasting away" her victims, this was a pretty efficient method of accomplishing that.

*

I had never intended for a single moment to give it up to Dirk Farrell for a $600 loan. I was just playing a desperate game and he'd forced my hand. After all, we'd only been together again for a couple of weeks and he hadn't regained my trust; I had no intention of doing the nasty with him for love *or* money. So I was far from emotionally broken-hearted by the rejection of an offer that wasn't sincere. What had pissed me off in the diner was his refusal of my *pretend* offer. This was a less painful defeat, like when someone gives their boyfriend a "Does He Love You" quiz from Cosmo and they flunk.   But still, my pride was wounded. There I was, practically groveling at his feet, offering my SELF, the all-the-way promise of his fantasies fulfilled, and he said *no*? So that he could keep his money and get a guitar sooner instead of having little ol' grateful me in his bed? I felt humiliated to have the offer of my long-guarded and old-fashioned virginity passed up for a G & L Bluesboy Sunburst....even if I hadn't had the slightest intention of pulling through with it.

So, with Farrell punking out on his "ends of the earth" routine, and with the events in my family providing more than enough motivation, I had less than a week to put my last and most desperate plan into action.

With Sean and Pat still in the hospital, the first part of Plan C turned out to be easier to pull off than I'd expected. A few days after the accidents, I came home after dark to a relatively empty house. Dad and Brian were already at visiting hours, Mike was watching TV with a bag of Doritos.

"Hey Mike! Going to the hospital tonight?"

"Already been," he said laconically. "I'll take you tomorrow if you want."

"K," I replied. "Where's Dylan?"

"Up in his room." He didn't take his eyes off the screen.

"Did you guys eat?"

"Not hungry," he was sounding a little annoyed. I could tell he wanted to be left alone or he'd have paused the digital cable. He stuffed some more Doritos in his mouth. "Dylan made himself a pizza."

I went to the front of the house to the

kitchen. A torn box was lying on the counter next to the microwave. I dabbed off some tomato sauce from the door with a paper towel. Dylan had indeed holed himself up in his room with one of his cardboard pizzas and a noisy video game. I heard it all the way through his door as I snuck up the stairs.

Avoiding the creaking step at the top, I hit the landing and shuddered as I noted the dark stain still visible in the center of the hall from the Halloween ivy incident. The stain looked like some kind of alien mold. It was black and copper-maroon where my blood had mixed with the smashed spiders and Sean's glassy mess. I turned my head from it and ducked into Mike and Pat's bedroom.

Their room was an homage to sports, shelves stuffed with souvenir signed balls, pennants, and trophies from grammar school victories. Field hockey, baseball, soccer, basketball. You name it, the twins had tried it. I felt as cold as the marble and metal trophy columns lining their shelves and I wanted to run. I wasn't happy about what I was about to do but the stain in the hall had only reminded me of why I had to continue.

I walked determinedly to Mike's desk. He always kept his wallet in the top drawer when he wasn't using it. Top desk drawer. Duh. Might as well have put a little engraved invitation for burglars right on the blotter. I scribbled down the numbers and the security code from his credit card and walked back downstairs breathlessly to my room where I went online to book a flight with it.

This is truly a desperate move, I thought as I typed in the flight details. Mike was going to kill me. But that would come later. The bill wouldn't come until December and I'd be gone and back by then with a promise to work it off in indentured servitude for life if need be. My hands trembled over the keys.

I rummaged in my own desk for my passport, now doubly glad that Dad had taken me and Dylan with him on a business trip to London after mom died.

There was one more thing. I still needed cash for the trip. I was happy to stay at a youth hostel but they weren't exactly free. Plus, I knew there'd be other expenses. I had a little bank account I could trash but not enough for a room and transportation to and from the airports and getting around Dublin. Who knew what else I'd need to hunt down my "Dorian Grey" auntie? I didn't want to get deported for vagrancy and begging in the streets before I had a chance to accomplish my mission.

So I had no choice but to play Farrell.

*

It was the Tuesday before Thanksgiving. My flight left the next night. I planned it that way so I wouldn't miss too much school and because I knew it would be easy to get Farrell to consider cutting the half day of classes before Turkey Day. I had already spent an entire week being so extra nice to him that I was popping Tums to stop myself from getting sick to my stomach.

meet me after sch at tennis cts

I texted him in Bio where it was easy to hide the phone under the big lab desks.

"What's up, Bran?" he said, crunching across the dead leaves and gravel on the path outside the school entrance as he approached me after dismissal. I was leaning on the chain link fence waiting for him.

"I have a surprise for you," I said in a low voice, slipping my hands into his open coat and around his waist. "Could I possibly get you to ditch classes with me tomorrow?"

"What have you got in mind?"

"Weeeeellllll..." I stuck my hands in his jeans pockets and pulled him even closer. "I've been thinking."

"Uh, oh. That's dangerous."

"No, seriously. I've been thinking about...us. About how close we're getting. I...I want to spend the day with you tomorrow. Alone." I turned my face up to him and brushed his nose with mine affectionately.

"Sounds like a plan. But what brought this on? Didn't your Dad give you hell when you cut to come see me in the hospital?"

"Yes....but this time I'd like to come see you in *another* bed," I said, running my fingers through his hair, behind his ear and down his neck. "You know what I mean?"

I looked up in his eyes as if they contained the whole world but, for a moment, I thought that I saw confusion in them. Oh, please! Don't let him question me! I was feeling all kinds of guilty already and if he questioned me I knew I might blow it.

"Ohhh!" he said as the confusion gave way to a grin so wide it threatened to move off the boundaries of his face. "Wow! Sure!" He tucked his hand under my chin and pulled my mouth to his.

That was it. Easy. No explanation necessary. No need to beg or to tell him how handsome he was or how hot I was for him; being a guy, he already took all that for-granted.

"Well, your Dad will be at work for sure," I continued quickly, setting up the scenario before he could propose anything that didn't fit my plans. "At my place there's no telling who goes and stays. Especially lately. So, park your car on the corner of Hillside and wait for me to ditch my ride. We can go to your house and...you know." I stood up on my toes and kissed him again.

He looked puzzled again but only for a moment.

"I...I just don't understand what brought this on."

Had he been, say, a girl, I would have been concerned that he might have been considering my offer as a bid for comfort and escape from the strain of having banshees after your family and two brothers on the brink of death. Had he been my guidance counselor, I would have been worried that he might be wondering whether my offer was a decision born of emotional distress that I should reconsider. But, as a regular guy, my worry was that he was contemplating the more glaringly obvious possibility that I might be laying – no pun intended – the ground work for hitting him up for a loan a second time. Was that crossing his mind? I hadn't mentioned it once since the diner. I'd been an extra sweet girlfriend. Had I overplayed it?

"I want you, baby," I said breathlessly. "I'm ready, and I want you to be the one." Still under the cover of his open coat, I worked my hands to the front and teasingly inched them just inside his belt buckle. He smiled back. Whatever had crossed his mind seemed to have made a quick exit down a side synapse and his hormones had taken over.

Chapter 5 – Fooling Farrell

Without my purpose in mind, without my bottled up anger, fooling Farrell might have been more difficult, but I'd been furious with him ever since he'd failed to pull through for me on the loan. Yes, it was a lot to ask. But I tend to take things people say literally and I wouldn't tell someone I'd be there for them "no matter what" if I didn't mean it. And I certainly wouldn't hold out money from a friend who needed it to stop a red-eyed fiend from offing her whole family. So I was angry, and the last thing I was feeling was all gooey amorous for Dirk Farrell. But I had to bite the bullet and put on an act for the sake of my brothers. It had been over ten days since Sean had said a word or opened his eyes and the image of his face, so pale and white against the only slightly lighter linens, haunted me as much as the white faces of the banshees.

It was that image that had given me the will to go against my conscience. I was at once ashamed and proud of the way I'd been pulling things off. I didn't like to use anyone, and I did care for Farrell in spite of his faults. But he'd been the one to give me a little taste of what being used and betrayed felt like when he'd dumped me, so I kept justifying my actions, my inner dialogue reminding me that, if someone had to be played, well, Farrell could stand being knocked down a peg or two.

All these thoughts roiled in my brain Wednesday morning as I bolted down my breakfast hastily. I'd forgotten an important detail that had to be taken care of.

"I'll go get my things," I said, shoving the last bite of waffle down my throat and rising to bring my dish to the sink.

"Put a move on, Bridget," Dad said impatiently, "I want to get in early today."

"Umm...I have to go to the bathroom," I replied as I moved towards the door.

Dad sighed audibly. "I hate to tell you to be quick about it but...be quick about it," he called after me.

I made my way down the hall, shut the bathroom door behind me, and pulled out my cell phone.

VIP = do not call house 2day! will explain later b

It was for Celeste. Celeste was my only female friend in school, partly because she was about the only other girl in Dover High that wasn't into gangsta rap. Farrell was probably calling in sick for me at the same moment. Old Mrs. Van Houten, the attendance officer at school, knew I had no mom, so faking it myself wasn't even in the realm of possibility but, with all the men in my house, Farrell could pull it off.

In spite of the time crunch, Dad dropped me off at the end of the tennis courts before the one way turn across Highland and down White that all the slogging high school traffic had to take. I'd already cut once and Dad was not the type to forget that sort of thing. He'd have held my hand and walked me to the door if he could.

I could feels Dad's eyes burrowing in my back as I left the car. It was a tough situation. I didn't want to get too near the door. If Crabface saw me and I didn't show up to her first period class it would ruin everything. Damn the snail-like traffic! I fumbled around in my backpack looking for some tissues, stalling as much as I could.

Dad's car crawled ahead. The mom in the old Chevy in front of my dad suddenly stopped short and leaned on her horn. She scudded across the front seat and waved a book out the window. A thin Asian girl in a purple windbreaker ran to retrieve it. As I watched the scene I noticed that Dad's attention was not on the Asian girl; his head was turned around and his neck was craning my way. Damn! I used the tissues to pick imaginary gum off the bottom of my sneaker. It was either that or go into a very suspicious, movie-like slow motion.

I was still fussing with my shoe when Celeste caught sight of me and gave me all the excuse I needed to stop short of the school building for a few more minutes as Dad's car disappeared.

"Hey! How are the boys doing?" She twisted a streak of fuchsia hair off her face.

"About the same. Pat started running a fever. Sean seems...." I shrugged. My voice trailed off. It hurt to talk about them. I wadded up the tissues and stuffed them into a side pocket of my pack.

"What's up with the text message, Brandy? Why are you going all James Bond and shit on me?"

"Listen, Celeste, I really need you to cover for me until around ten tonight. I told Dad we're

89

working on a paper after school. He's going to be home, getting things ready for dinner tomorrow. I usually help but I told him we *really* had to work so, whatever you do, stay away from the house."

"What am I covering for?" she said, eyeing me with concern. "You're not running away are you?"

Celeste had run away when she was a freshman because her Dad had smacked her for piercing her own nose with a needle and an ice cube. She'd hid out all night in the White Castle until one of the cashiers had gotten suspicious and called the cops. All the counseling afterwards had turned her into an amateur psychiatrist with everybody else. If she thought I was running away she might even rat me out. Puking sliders for a whole day after her own experience had left her with a Pavlovian aversion to solving your problems that way.

"No, nothing like that." I hoped I sounded confident and convincing.

The first bell rang.

"Let's go," said Celeste, turning towards the building.

"No. I'm...I'm meeting Farrell. His dad's out of town and we're going to hang out all day at his house."

Celeste's entire demeanor changed.

"Ohhhhhh! I get it," she said with a twinkle in her eye. "Old Catholic Brandy finally gettin' ready to get down with it?"

"Ummmm...," was my vague reply, playing into a fact of human nature: People believe what they want to believe. I didn't have to say a word.

My alibi was sealed.

She winked at me as I headed down towards Hillside. I winked back and she gave me a thumbs up. Whew.

*

You would think booze would be easy to get in an Irish family, but not at the Connors. Mike and Pat always had a couple of six packs in the fridge but they kept track of them. (If their underage siblings wanted beer they'd have to get it like they did when they were underage, and bribe someone else's older brother.) Anyway, I needed something stronger, something sure fire. And I needed it on short notice. I wound up taking a tip from the twins, paying Los's older brother to get me a big bottle of cheap vodka and a fifth of Captain Morgan. They were both in the pack I now laid down gently on the floor of Farrell's car.

"Hey! How's my girl?" Farrell said, running a hand across my hair. I couldn't tell if his expression was affectionate or cocky, there was some kind of odd gleam in his eye. I decided to assume cockiness since it would make what I was about to do easier.

"Great!" My voice cracked just a little. I looked down, hoping he would take it as nervousness, which it was, but not for the reason he might have suspected.

We were half way to his house when he smacked his hand on the steering wheel, yelled "Shit!", and almost scared the same out of me.

"What?"

"I forgot to call Van Hootie!"

I opened my mouth to call Farrell a dumb ass but I had to keep things cool between us, so I just rubbed my hand on his thigh and muttered something lame about making the day worth all the trouble I was going to get into.

We were at his house in no time, a big, white colonial on a block with a lot of nosy neighbors. As Farrell struggled with the dead bolt, I glanced around to see if any of them were around and bounced up and down on my toes as I waited, doing the cold dance.

"C'mon, Farr. I'm ffff...frr..freezing."

"Don't worry, Bran. I'll warm you right up in a few minutes," he said lecherously as the door slid open. A blast of warm air hit me in the face and Farrell's smoky grey cat, Monterey, dashed past us into the yard.

"I have a little surprise for you," I said as we climbed straight up the stairs that faced the front entrance.

"And I have one for you, too," he replied, opening the door of his room. I stopped dead. Farrell's usually scuzzy room was transformed. It was as if Tinkerbell had brought her entire colony to visit. Tiny little lights twinkled everywhere. He had strung white Christmas lights around his bed and draped more across the windows and over the curtain rods. There were at least fifteen of those supermarket candles in glasses with pictures of the Virgin Mary and the Sacred Heart of Jesus set about the floor. But they were all painted pink.

"I tried to paint over the glass so that the saints wouldn't be staring at us," he said sheepishly, "but you can still sort of see the images when they're lit. Is that okay? Do you...do you like it?"

Crap!   Farrell was being sweet and romantic. Just what I didn't need. And he'd gone through a great deal of effort. He'd even picked up all the trash and dirty socks from his floor. Damn! Why couldn't he say something stupid to turn me off?

"It's...it's just so...so..." I couldn't face him so I put my arm around his waist and gave him a quick hug sideways, "sweet of you. It's lovely, Farr."

He grinned like a little kid who had just finished reciting his ABCs. "I....I wanted it to be special for you, Brandy. I know it's your first time."

I know he meant well, but that sentence did the trick of pissing me off. If he'd just left it at "special" or had said "for us" it would not have ruined my mood. But the "for you" and the rest of it reminded me that *he'd* already done this before with Lisa DeLotto, right after we broke up. She'd lost no time in blabbing the news all over school either, as if she'd won some kind of first-one-to-nail-the-ex-boyfriend contest.   Farrell had taken a lot of crap about it from his friends who all called her "whipped cream cheese" (because she was "so spreadable") and he never admitted to more than a one night stand, but it still pissed me off to think about it.

"Well, thank you," I whispered, forcing down the anger that had started to well up again.

"Now, where's *your* surprise?"

I unzipped my book bag slowly and his

eyes widened, only to register a little bit of disappointment when I pulled out the bottles.

"What's the matter, I thought you liked Captain Morgan?"

He laughed a low, snuffly kind of laugh.

"I....I was kind of hoping you were going to pull out...lingerie."

Like Lisa DeLotto? I thought. *What did that little tramp wear when you had her up here? Have you even changed your nasty sheets since then? Oh, keep going, Farrell,* I thought. *You're making this easier by the minute.*

"Oh," I said softly, trying to sound wounded. I kind of was.

"But rum's good too!" he chirped, grabbing the bottle from my hand. "What's with the vodka? You know I hate vodka."

Actually, I did, and had counted on that fact. "Oh! That's mine. I had some last Christmas at Uncle Ian's and I really liked it," I fibbed. *Besides*, I thought, *it was the best choice for switching with water without you noticing.*

"Well, maybe we should hit that first?"

"You just said you hated vodka."

"Well, just one. Together. Like a toast maybe?"

"NO! Um, I mean, no...you shouldn't mix. It will make you sick. And I want you to enjoy your rum. I went through a lot of trouble to get it for you." I fiddled with the collar of his shirt and pulled him down for a kiss. He pushed the coat off my shoulders and slid his hands under my tee shirt against the skin on my back.

"Mmmmmmm...maybe we should save all the booze for later," he said shoving his hand further up towards my bra closure.

"No. It's my very first time, Farr. I'm nervous. The vodka will relax me."

"You know, Bran, you're full of surprises. I mean, you act so tough on the outside but, inside, you're still a little girl"

It took a concerted effort on my part not to stick my finger down my throat, an action that would have more closely demonstrated my true feelings. Instead, I smiled, handed him the rum, kicked off my sneakers, and sank into the battered bean bag chair on the floor.

"Why don't you come up here next to me?" he said, patting the fuzzball infested dark green blanket on his bed.

"I'm good down here awhile *(where you can't ask me why my vodka has no smell)*. I want to get a little buzz on first. I'll come up after I've had," I held the bottle up so he could see its ample size, "maybe half the bottle."

"Half the bottle?" Farrell went into an exaggerated fit of laughter.

Perfect.

"Yes, half the bottle," I said defensively.

"Brandy, you'll be completely trashed after a half a bottle. Do you remember what happened at Ron's party last summer?" I clearly recalled throwing my guts up after three beers at one of our drummer's keggers and had counted on Farrell's memory of vomit all over his new boots to elicit this reaction.

"Yeah, so? That was a mistake. I ate something bad at the mall before I went. I had food poisoning or something. I can hold my liquor. I bet I can drink more than you can."

The hysterical laughter began anew. "God, you're funny, Bran! You're so full of...." He stopped, took a look at my expression, and shut up. No guy wants to piss you off when he thinks he's about to get some. He cracked the seal, tilted back a draught of the Captain, wiped his mouth with the back of his hand, and continued in a slightly condescending tone. "Okay, Brandy, we'll keep drinking, and you just tell me when you're buzzed."

I nodded. I knew Farrell. He wasn't going to let me beat him after I'd thrown down the verbal gauntlet. He didn't have to agree to a drinking contest but I knew we were in one.

He put his iPod into its cradle and started to play some tunes as I twisted off the carefully resealed cap of my bottle. As if to challenge me, he chugged down a few more shots. I slugged back a drink, coughing for effect. A sly smile cracked one corner of Farrell's mouth.

"You okay, Bran?"

"Fine! Just fine."

We sat there with tension in the air. The tension of sex and challenge. We were walking the fine line between losing our inhibitions and losing our lunch.

"Just don't go passing out on me, Bran."

"I won't. Puking would spoil the romance."

Farrell threw back another drink. I tilted my head back too but cut it short and forced a little girly cough again, not wanting to arouse suspicion. We sat for a while talking about the band and music, two subjects Dirk never tired of; I listened as if in rapt attention and sipped patiently.

"Daft Punk is probably the best electronic mushic ever," he slurred finally. I hoped that my face did not reveal the glimmer of hope that his mispronunciation kindled.

His own registered surprise as he stared down at me.

"How're you doin' with that, Bran?"

I held up the bottle. About a quarter was gone.

"Fine. Great! How about you?"

"Oh, me too. I'm jes' fine." He sank a little lower down on his headboard and rubbed his stomach. His lids closed a moment but he fought off the sensation of drowsiness.

"Wouldn't you like to mix something with that vodka? There's shum juice downstairs."

"No. No, straight is good for me. If you want to cut the taste of your rum or something though, go ahead and get some soda." It was easy to squeeze a little condescension into my voice.

He took a long slug.

"C'mere and let's make out," he said as he finished. "Don't you have a buzz on yet?"

I made a thoughtful face, as if I was examining my condition for any effects. "Maybe a little."

"Damned Irish," cursed Farr under his breath.

"What's that?"

"I said...damn...I wish...I wish you'd come up here and sit next to me."

"Well, let me just have one more drink." I took a good long one. Farrell tipped back his bottle and did the same.

97

At this point Farrell lost his taste - or his capacity - for conversation. His eyes grew heavy and I could see he was starting to sail down the river into the land of the trashed, at least two sheets to the wind. . *Slow him down, Bran,* I thought. *You don't want him dead of alcohol poisoning, just passed out.*

"Bathroom break," I announced, jumping up from the bean bag chair. Once inside, I decided to dawdle in order to give the alcohol in Farrell's blood some time to work before he killed himself trying to beat me in a game that I knew was rigged. I examined the cute Sponge Bob Dixie cups in the dispenser. Washed my hands. Twice. Snooped in the medicine cabinet. Opened the vanity. There, in the top drawer, was a hot pink scrunchie. I lifted it up and felt the fire in my face as I noted a few blonde hairs caught in the elastic. Traces of Lisa DeLotto? I turned around and made an exit, fully intent on resuming my bogus drinking immediately and momentarily losing my moral concern that Farrell might drop dead.

Fortunately, when I reached the foot of his bed, he was sound asleep.

Chapter 6 – Not Only Fairies Fly

The airport terminal was bizarre. JFK was confusing, and all the little ordinary annoyances of travel were exacerbated by my worries. I felt like I was stuck in an old sci-fi story about a traveler lost in time, trapped in a queue with crying babies, waiting with a bunch of people who didn't use deodorant for a plane that would never come. Or, who knows, maybe my fellow travelers had applied deodorant but they'd waited on line so long it had worn off? There were the blank stares of the travel weary, the vapid gazes of the zombie-like super-economy passengers trying to make their third connecting flight. And me. Essentially a runaway. Every TSA agent that passed made my stomach turn.

But I felt some satisfaction at having pulled it off, especially since the whole plan had almost fallen apart. I had plenty of time to think about it in the nearly endless line to the ticket counter.

Finding Farrell asleep in his bed was just what I'd wanted. I'd lifted his limp hand, shook him, and called his name but he snored on. So I started to search his room for the money. That had been my intent and, from the looks of him, I figured I'd have plenty of time to find it before I'd have to worry about him waking and discovering my crime. Would he call the cops on me when he did? I hadn't thought about that. I checked the contents of the bottle leaning up on his hip. Just about the halfway point. Hopefully, this would buy me enough time to do everything I had to do before he awoke.

I searched all the obvious places first. Sock drawer. Night stand. The closet (where I discovered what he'd done with all his dirty clothes). I tore through the pile of laundry, broken CDs and crumpled papers without success, shut the door, and went to look under the bed where dust bunnies had reproduced so prolifically it was almost pornographic. Nothing.

After about forty minutes I really started to worry. *Wow,* I thought, *he's smarter than I gave him credit for.* I dragged his desk chair to the window and almost broke my neck searching the rod pocket of the nubby drapes, the dust so thick I almost fell off my perch from coughing. By around 10 a.m. I was standing in the center of the room feeling helpless. Then Farrell snorted and I turned to the bed.

The bed? Oh, no! It couldn't be, could it? Would Farrell be so dumb as to hide the money under the mattress? I made a pained face. He'd been sleeping soundly as I'd moved around the room searching like a cat burglar, but moving him? That might be another story.

I stole over, knelt down, slid my arms between the mattress and box spring, and slowly ran them along the edge. Nothing. But I couldn't be sure because there was no way to get all the way to the middle without waking him. I stood up and tapped my foot. It had to be in there; I'd looked everywhere else. Jacket pockets. Bookshelf. Lucky for me, he wasn't much of a reader, just a few school texts and graphic novels. Jeans pockets. Shirt pockets. I was starting to get desperate. He'd once told me he was hiding the money in his room. Damn! Where would Farrell hide money he was saving for a new guitar?

The guitar!

I ran to the closet and creaked open the door a second time. Why didn't I think of that? I'd already opened the electric guitar case. I'd searched it for loose linings and looked inside the little storage box inside. But he had another guitar. I pushed all the laundry aside in the closet and dug out the worn case that housed his old, seldom-used acoustic. The guitar was battered and sported nylon strings. His grandpa had given it to him in seventh grade and, even though he'd outgrown it, I'd seen him treat it like a priceless Stradivarius the few times he'd taken it out. Clearly, its value was only sentimental.

I went to the window, pulled aside the drapes, held the guitar up to the light, and saw the envelope duct-taped inside next to the sound hole. Nice going. No burglar would take the old acoustic with an electric case nearby. But now there was the matter of the racket that would occur if the current thief tried to stick her hand in the sound hole and yank out the fat envelope from between the strings.

I walked to the hall, snatching a blanket that was folded on an old chest at the foot of the bed on the way, then crept downstairs and sat on the bottom step. Laying the blanket across the sound hole for good measure, I began to turn the tuning keys carefully, loosening the strings one by one until I'd removed three of them, slid my hand inside, and peeled off the envelope. Victory!

Then I tiptoed back up the stairs, pulled

the wad of tissues that I'd use earlier to wipe the pretend gum off my shoe from my back pack pocket, and snuck down again. I wadded the tissue into the money envelope until it was reasonably fat and stuck it back on inside the sound hole. Now all I had to do was replace the strings and return the guitar to the closet. I was tightening the second string and feeling pretty self-satisfied when:

BAM! BAM! BAM! Ding dong!

My heart leapt to my throat. Farrell's front door was the kind that had six little glass panes across the top and I saw a head trying to peer over them. I thought I recognized the receding hairline. Or was it my imagination? I ducked down and crawled across the floor to the front of the living room by the windows, raising my eyes slowly above the sill. I shot back down in a millisecond. Dad's car was right out front! Crap! Crap, shit, damn, poopie and every other curse word I'd ever used in my life!

BAM! BAM! Ding dong!

Don't wake up, Farrell, I prayed softly. *Don't wake up.*

I knew Dad and, because I did, I was afraid he'd break down the door. *Think, Brandy, think!*

I pulled out my cell phone. *Celeste.* She had the early lunch period and she often cut out to the pizzeria. There was a chance. I crawled to the dining room and hit her number. It rang once, twice. If she was in school and couldn't talk, her voice mail would pick up the fourth time.

"Heeeeeeeeyyyy, girl, how's it goin'? Why you callin' me instead of doin' Uh! Uh! Uh! with...."

I rolled my eyes. "Listen, Celeste, I'll tell you later but this is really important. My dad's at Farrell's front door."

BAM! BAM!

"Dirk Farrell! Open up the door this instant or I'll break it down!" I heard him clearly from two rooms away. The whole neighborhood probably heard him.

"Shit, Bran, that's awful! Are you naked?"

"No! Yes! Never mind! He *can't* find us. Here's his number. You got a pen?"

"His number? What am I supposed to do with..."

"DO YOU HAVE A PEN?" It was a shouting whisper.

"Okay! Okay! Yeah but..."

"555-347-6785. Got that?"

Ding dong!

"Yeah...555-347-6785."

"Call him. NOW! Tell him..." Thoughts in my brain rolled like an Atlantic City slot machine and hit upon an ugly but possibly winning combination. "Tell him that you're from St. Clare's hospital and he has to get there right away."

It was absolutely awful. But it was the only thing I could think of at the moment. The possibility of one of my brothers' decline versus putting a temporary kibosh on the inevitable and eventual loss of his daughter's virginity. Which would win in Dad roulette? My money was on another health crisis.

"I don't know, Bran. That's a little radical, dontcha think?"

The bell rang yet again and Dad yelled

something incoherent. Probably another one of his Irish curses.

"Celeste! What's more radical? A fake call from the hospital or...or my dad finding me naked in Farrell's bed? And you owe me! Who covered for you when you were going out with LaMonte Johnson? Do you want me to tell your dad what you said about his...."

"Okay, Bran! Okay! Wow! Blackmail. You must be desperate."

"Just be vague. They never tell you much over the phone from a hospital. And hang up quick after you tell him. Don't give him time to ask questions."

I sank under the dining room table with tears in my eyes and watched an ant crawl across the scuffed oak floor. I felt lower than that.

Dad was still pounding on the door. What if a neighbor came? *She's in there with him, the little slut! I saw them this morning from the window while I was watching television. I looked out and they were right here on this porch.* And what if Celeste couldn't pull it off? What if she called him from inside the luncheonette and he heard voices? Or out on the sidewalk and a car honked and he got suspicious?

"Farrell! I know you're in there!"

What if Farrell woke up, came down the stairs in a drunken stupor and fell over the guitar lying at the bottom and broke his neck? Could I be convicted of manslaughter? I crawled back to the living room where I could see the stairs and squeezed my eyes shut, willing with all my heart for Farrell to stay asleep.

Deedly-dee dee! Deedly-dee dee!

Dad's lame ring tone went off.

"Hello!" I heard him answer more brusquely than normal. Then there was some muttering. I heard him shift his feet at the doorstep, as if deciding what to do. My heart was right up next to my uvula, pounding like one of Ron's drum solos. Finally, I heard footsteps run down the porch stairs. A door slammed. A car started.

I crawled back to the front window. He was gone. I padded over in my stocking feet to the guitar, hopped over it and tiptoed back up the stairs. The lights were still twinkling softly in the room. Everything was in place. Farr was still passed out. The only thing that had changed was that now he was on his stomach and his face was hanging down over the floor above a copious amount of vomit - all over the sneakers I'd left sitting next to his bedside. *Okay. Fair enough*, I thought. *Payback for Ron's kegger incident and the ruined Italian leather boots.*

I made my way back down, hastily strung the last string and settled the guitar back in its case in the closet. Then I blew out the candles, pulled the plug on the lights – not wanting arson added to my list of crimes - grabbed my things, and put the note I'd hoped would throw him off track on the nightstand:

Love you, baby. We both got trashed and fell asleep. Had to get home.

I finally let myself out and onto the porch with a small sigh of relief. Monterey whizzed past me, the door almost catching his tail as I locked it behind me with a snap. I rummaged for my cell phone in my pockets, wondering if I could afford to spend some of Farrell's money to call a cab. Rats! I'd left it on the dining room floor! *Relax, Bran, the phone won't work in Ireland anyway.*

I walked down the wooden steps to the narrow walkway and turned down the street. Mission accomplished. Now all I had to do was make it home on foot before Dad got there.

*

I couldn't believe I was on my way to Dublin. The drone of the jet engine was the white noise background to my own song of hope. I was sitting in the not-so-surprisingly-cramped seat of Continental flight 156 with one more reason to be glad of my decision. Dad was in the hospital. And it wasn't for a visit. I crumpled the letter I'd just read in my hand and wiped the tears from my eyes. What if my idea didn't work?

I stared out the window into the darkness. A wisp of white cloud in the distance made me shudder. I pulled down the shade and tried to sleep but the events of the day kept running through my head.

As I'd made my way home from Farrell's, I worried if I'd blown it all. My plan had been to go home, pick up my suitcase, and be on the train to Manhattan by three, before anyone got home and long before Dad could find the note I was going to stuff under his pillow for him to discover at bedtime. If my connecting shuttle at Penn Station was on time and there were no delays, I'd arrive at the airport with plenty of time to check in for my flight.

But if Dad was waiting for me at the house there would surely be a delay. A *huge* delay. Maybe a locked-in-my-room-with-rented-guard-dogs-in-the-yard delay. Maybe a pack-of-nuns-waiting-to-take-me-to-the-convent delay. I tried not to think of the consequences as I hobbled over the little pieces of invisible gravel and stone that my cold feet seemed to find with every step. The benign scar from the Halloween incident had not been hurting but now it felt like an icy piece of glass was still stuck inside.

Dad's car wasn't in sight on either side of the street when I turned the corner but I couldn't be sure he wasn't home. Any house big enough for seven people is big enough for a garage. Then I noticed another problem. Mike's car was in the driveway. Huh? Maybe Dad had put out the word when he'd discovered I'd cut. Damn our efficient attendance officer! Did old Mrs. Van Houten tell Dad that Farrell and I had both cut? Is that how he learned where I was or was I becoming transparent? Transparent, I figured. It's illegal to rat out someone else's kid. I crossed the street and ducked behind Mr. Gomez's electrical truck to watch the front door.

I waited impatiently, lightly stamping on the damp, dried grass near the curb to keep my feet moving, suspecting that in another few minutes I'd never be able to make it to the train station on time. I leaned out from behind the van, ready to make a run for it, cringing at the thought of climbing over the bushes to my room without shoes on. It was soon evident that I wouldn't have to because, as I peered out from

Mr. Gomez van, Mike burst from the front door, got in his car, and took off like someone had just told him he had an interview to pitch for the Yankees in ten minutes.

As soon as his car turned the corner, I ran to the front door, unlocked it, and bolted down the hall to my room. My feet were screaming.

It took a minute to pull off my damp, dirty socks and throw on some nice, thick, fresh ones and clean shoes. Then I dragged my packed suitcase off the closet shelf, ripped open the Hefty bag that gave it that still-in-storage look, slung the tote with my train pass, plane tickets, some gum, and snacks for the flight over my shoulder, and ran towards the door.

I almost didn't see the note on my dresser, propped up against the half-burnt candle next to the funeral parlor holy picture. It was just a folded sheet of paper with my name across the front in Mike's handwriting.

No time to read this now, I thought. Probably a lecture anyway. Something along the lines of: *Dad told me you cut classes today and might have been with Farrell! Shame on you!* I just wasn't in the mood. I grabbed it and stuffed it in my tote. Then I took the steps to Dad's room two at a time to shove my own note under his pillow.

About fifty seconds before the train pulled out I reached the Dover train station and my epic marathon of nerves and rush commenced in earnest, dissolving into a mental checklist of tickets, plans, and belongings, with a major portion also devoted to picking my cuticles and worrying about what I had done. When I finally got to Penn Station there was the hassle of dragging my bag through the crowds for over a city block to the hotel where the Airlink stopped, a van full of travelers chattering about their respective destinations, the epic line waiting to check in at JFK, the fear of being pulled out of said line by the police dragging me to the station for theft and credit card fraud. I had a lot on my mind and didn't give Mike's letter another thought until I was sitting in the plane. The moment the engines started I reached into my bag for some gum to keep my ears from popping and spied the crumpled paper shoved down the side. Did I want to ruin the flight, I pondered? Oh well, might as well face the music and get it over with.

I opened the note slowly and smoothed the wrinkles out on my lap as the plane began to roll down the tarmac. My heart picked up speed along with the plane as I read:

Dear Bran,

I've been trying to get you for over an hour. You aren't at school (we'll talk about that later) and you're not answering your phone. I don't know what's up but as soon as you get this call me. I hate to tell you this way but Dad's in the hospital. It's a MILD heart attack. MILD, I swear it. He showed up to visit the boys and passed out in the lobby. Right place. Who says the Connors aren't lucky? CALL ME as soon as you get home just so I don't worry about you.

Mike

For a moment I pictured myself jumping

up and shouting "Stop the plane!" like I was in a movie. But I couldn't move. I couldn't breathe. I just sat there with my hand over my mouth, not knowing if the empty, pukey feeling in my stomach was from take off or Mike's news or both.

What had I done?

*

I couldn't sleep. I was on a red-eye and there was absolutely nothing to see outside the widow so I was staring at the plastic shade in the dark. The airplane on the little map on the back of the seat in front of me kept lurching forward in tiny increments as if the plane had arthritis and was on a walker. I didn't want to listen to music or watch a movie or the old I Love Lucy reruns, even though they never failed to make me laugh. I just sat there full of Sunday Catechism guilt. How could I laugh when my brothers and Dad were in the hospital?

Dad. In the hospital. Had I put him there myself? All that pounding on the door and shouting. Why couldn't I have thought of something besides cutting class to accomplish my goal? I should have known he'd catch me. I bet he had called Mrs. Van Houten himself, to check on me.

What the hell had gotten into me? I'd pulled some stupid shit in my time but this was truly nuts. I was traveling on a plane with a ticket I'd bought with my brother's stolen credit card. And I was carrying cash money I'd stolen from my boyfriend.

Your EX-boyfriend, Bran, I corrected myself. He was never going to speak to me again when he finally discovered the theft. Maybe I could blame it on Lisa DeLotto?

Crap! I suddenly realized I'd forgotten the half-full bottle of faux vodka on the bean bag chair. *Ah, well,* I sighed, *the cop shows always say that every criminal leaves a trail behind.* He'd be pretty certain of my guilt if he took a slug. I wondered if he had woken up yet or if he had thrown up again and choked on his own vomit like in the news stories about frat parties gone wrong. Truancy. Theft. Treachery. Homicide. I was really racking it up.

The Indian couple in the seats next to me smelled of curry. It wasn't a terrible smell but I wasn't in the mood for food so it bothered me. The man was already snoring when I first got up to go to the bathroom. He looked very annoyed when I fell over his wife, onto his knees and into the aisle, waking him.

A stomach virus? Was that it? Nerves? Whatever it was, by the time I had tripped over the poor guy for the third time, I returned from the bathroom to find him in my window seat, leaning onto the interior wall of the plane and snoring more deeply than ever. I plopped myself down into the aisle seat and squirmed around for about a half an hour before I finally nodded off.

I was dreaming of green heaths and white cliffs when I woke up with a chill. I pulled the ratty airplane blanket and my coat around me more tightly. All the lights were out. I glanced over at the GPS. The little airplane was hobbling along over the Atlantic and just about everyone in it was sleeping.

Diagonally in front of me, an elderly woman with wispy yellow hair was wearing a blindfold, breathing open-mouthed with her head back and one arm hanging limply over the seat. To my right was a tall, snoozing giant whose lanky legs sprawled into the aisle, threatening to trip any groggy traveler searching in the dim cabin for the restroom. Then I made the mistake of looking over my shoulder at the seat behind him.

No amount of coats or blankets could have stopped the cold terror that ran through me when I saw the banshee. The horrible one. Her figure cloaked and hooded like the Grim Reaper, the outline of her skull visible behind her thin, white face. She stared straight ahead, rocking back and forth with her hands on her knees as if preparing to keen.

Hysterical aphasia. It is not a fun thing. It's when your voice fails you from fright. You try to scream. You want to scream. But the only thing that comes out of your mouth is air. Haaaaahhhhhhhhhhh. Haaaaaaaahhhhhhh. I'd read about it but this was the first time it happened to me. I must've looked a fright myself, sitting there with my eyes and mouth wide open in the dark, screaming silently.

Her face was white and empty as an overcast sky, and when her red eyes caught mine, she leaned forward and grinned hideously. I wanted to get up and run but I was riveted to the spot. I couldn't turn, couldn't shout, couldn't even peel my eyes off of her filmy features. She was smiling at me! Why? Triumph? Two of my brothers and my dad were hospitalized. Was this satisfaction? Or was she here displaying approval because she knew of my plans?

Before I could consider these questions, the woman whose seat the spirit had appropriated returned from the lavatory and the wraith vanished.

"What are you looking at?" the woman snapped before I realized I was still staring at her seat slack-jawed, the image of the banshee burnt into my mind like a white hot brand.

Chapter 7 -When Irish Eyes Are Crying

Dublin airport was much smaller than JFK and everything was in English but I might as well have been trying to read cuneiform in Uzbekistan for all the sense things made to me once I disembarked the red-eye. I had a total of about twenty minutes sleep and it was three a.m. in New Jersey: not a great time to perform complex tasks like finding your way around in a strange country. I wandered out of customs through the green doors designated for those with "No dangerous items/Arriving from outside the UK" (like someone would *admit* to having dangerous items? *"Excuse me, sir. Where's the exit for people WITH bombs and weapons?"*). Then I walked zombie-like out of the terminal and through a transportation station into a parking lot before doubling back through everything to the terminal again. How hard could it be to find a bright green, double-decker bus? I needed to sit down, gain my bearings, and have a good ol' American breakfast sandwich. But, if there was a MacDonald's inside, I was in too much of a fog to notice. I glanced around dumbly at souvenir shops, rental car agencies, and a currency exchange. The latter seemed the best place to start since the only place to sit was at the kiosk for the internet SurfBoxes where, for a few euro, I could rest a moment and try to piece my head together.

After getting over the shock of how little I

got in exchange for the bills I slipped through the window, I ran to the pcs, put some coins in the slot, and tried to e mail Mike. There must've been twelve false starts before I gave up and typed in: *I'm fine. In Dublin. Info is in note under Dad's pillow. Don't have phone. Please e mail me with news.* I felt like Western Union. Mike deserved better but I was spent. All my bold moves felt like nothing more than the product of desperation and foolhardiness, not good ol' Brandy guts. Tired and alone in a strange place, I no longer felt so daring or self-assured about my plan. I felt completely lost and doubt was rushing in to fill up all the empty places inside.

*

It had been ridiculously easy to find the shuttle once I finally got my crap together enough to simply ask someone where it was. The driver of the green double decker told me he'd let me know when my stop near the hostel came up. I thanked him and took a step towards the nearest seat, but I was already thinking of my mission.

"Do you have phone books in Ireland?" I said, turning back towards him.

"Oh, yes, we have phone books in Ireland. Running water too," he winked.

I must've turned eight shades of red. "I'm sorry. I didn't mean it that way. I just don't know what's different and what's the same here and I really need a phone book."

"Well, if the hostel doesn't have one, you can always go to the post office on Connell Street. They've got 'em there."

I sank into a single seat by a window, pressing my cheek against the cold glass, willing myself to stay awake for the announcement of my stop. The city looked bigger than I'd expected and I was already feeling discouraged by the time the driver shouted:

"Who's looking for Aston Quay?"

It was a short walk but, in my exhaustion, it felt like a half a mile instead of half a block. When I saw the yellow letters that said *Abigail's,* I smiled for the first time since I'd left New Jersey.

Reception was on the second floor, a cheery yellow room where a cute guy named Aaron told me where to stash my valuables, where the luggage storage was, the key procedures, and how to get through the security measures. A sweet woman named Agnes handed me a towel and told me how to pick up clean linens, what to do with the dirty ones, and what time free breakfast was served. I nodded blankly to everything they said and then blurted: "Do you have a phone book?" It was clear that my thought processes weren't up to computing more than one simple thing at a time.

Aaron blinked only barely before asking, "Business or residential?"

Even this confused me. "Both," I answered, not wanting to tax my brain with such a complex decision. He put two heavy volumes on the counter. I slung my tote over my back, scooped up the books in the crook of my arm, and dragged the lot into the lounge area.

It was both better and worse than I thought. First of all, during the long flight a tiny bit of rational thought had begun to seep into my brain: Would finding a Connor in Dublin be like trying to find a Patel in Mumbai? For the better part, I was relieved to find that there were only seventeen Connors in the Eircom white pages but, of course, none of them were listed as: Connor, Your Long Lost Relative Cursed by a Banshee. There were no Maggies or Megs. Two Marias. A few "M" Connors from outside of Dublin in places like Dun Laoghaire and Howth. Nothing jumped out at me at all. That was the worse part. The desperation and fear that had driven me to this point suddenly flooded over me like the wild Irish sea of Dad's stories.

Now what, bright girl? Do you call up seventeen Irish people and say...what? I was never any good at wheedling things out of people and blunt wasn't going to work with Maggie. She obviously didn't want company. Especially Connor company. She'd left home decades ago and even her own mother had discovered her whereabouts through nothing but sheer luck. She might have changed her name. Moved out of Dublin. Gotten married. Crap! If she looked eternally young she might have gotten married and changed her name *several* times.

I took deep, gulping breaths and swallowed hard. *Stay calm*, I told myself, going for the business pages. First I looked for "Tea Shops". Zip. There were four listings under "Tea Merchants" but they were all national brands like Barry's. I already knew "Restaurants" would be a wash. Five full pages and, aside from the obvious ethnic titles, it was anyone's guess as to what kind of establishment the names represented. There was nothing inspiring under "Caterers" or

"Bakeries" either. *I am royally screwed*, I thought. *I've done a million stupid things and, for what? I am never going to find Maggie. My brothers are going to die, my dad is going to die....*

Two dark marks formed where tears plopped onto the thin white pages. I glanced up, shaking like the last autumn leaf in the wind. There was only one other person in the room, a red-haired guy sitting by a laptop with headphones on. Aaron had disappeared into the back room. I ran up the stairs praying that every one of my roommates would be out for the day.

*

Five of the six beds in the dormitory style accommodations I'd chosen were messed up; I assumed the remaining neat one was my "Bed 4". The drapes were closed tightly and only one occupant was present. Her face was largely unidentifiably because it was veiled in a mass of flaming red hair and she was flat on her stomach, a loose-as-spaghetti arm hanging over one of the top bunks, mouth twisted against a pillow, drooling and snoring loudly. A note propped up against the lamp on the solitary bed stand read: "Charlotte. Drink lots of water when you get up. We'll be back for dinner."

Sleeping off a drunk. Good. I knew she wouldn't be able to hear my sobs but I stuffed my face into a pillow anyway as I threw myself onto the tidy bottom bunk in the corner.

I don't remember falling asleep. The next thing I was aware of was a tapping on the door.

Completely disoriented in the dimly lit room, I didn't know the time and was only vaguely aware of the day. Charlotte was still snoring and I figured it was one of her roommates. I jumped to answer but stopped about two feet from the door with my hand poised just over the handle.

Wouldn't her roommates have a key?

"Who is it?" My own voice sounded foreign to me.

"I'm looking for Miss Bridget Connor," said a high-pitched female voice.

My shoulders slumped in resignation. *This is it*, I figured. *My family has sent whatever the Irish equivalent of the police is after me and my ass is going to be on the next plane back to New Jersey. Time to face the music, Bran, and it isn't going to be "When Irish Eyes Are Smiling".* I went for the handle with mixed feelings of relief, defiance, and fear.

"Bridget Anne? Is that you dear?" said an adorable old lady in a raspberry cloche. The hat, decorated with a little feather bound under a tiny amber jewel, had a turned up brim that dipped down on one side and looked as if it was being worn for the first time. It was pulled down tightly over a neat mass of silvery curls, forming them into a frame around a face still beautiful in spite of its owner's age. A crisp, wool cape of a slightly deeper shade of fuchsia sported a gold stick pin and revealed a spill of white satin ruffles at the neck. Her lips were a soft magenta, her cheeks blushed with a tasteful wisp of pink; everything about the woman was perfectly, neatly, pulled together.

I was struck with a sudden awareness that

119

I hadn't had a shower in over a day and was still in the same clothes I had worn on the plane but my embarrassment immediately turned into utter humiliation when the strange woman threw her arms around my shoulders and hugged me. I was sure my 24-hour deodorant had expired 10 hours ago.

"Bridget! I'm yer great aunt, Molly!" She said, springing away to examine me at arms length. I hoped it was to get a better look and not a less better smell. "Oh, I'm *so* happy to meet yeh, dear, although I must say that I'd prefer it to have been under better circumstances."

I didn't know what to say. I was still tired and steeped in that dopey sort of feeling you get when you've been awakened suddenly from a deep sleep - which I had been.

"Aunt Molly?"

"Yer great aunt, dear. I'm yer grandfather Peter's younger sister. I live in Dun Laoghaire, just outside o' Dublin. I'd have been here sooner but I was stayin' with Aidan up north. Terrible thing about his boy." She folded her hands in front of her and put her head down, distancing herself from me momentarily. "As they say: 'Death is in front of an old person and at a young person's back.' It was a shock in spite of...." She stopped and seemed to pull herself together as neatly as her outfit. "Never mind that. Yeh've got worries of yer own I understand. Yer grandmother contacted Aidan when your family found out where you were headed and I came home straight away. My luggage is downstairs. I spoke with a delightful woman named Agnes at the desk and got them to refund four of yer five nights and made yer cancellation. Now get yer things and come downstairs and we'll drag everythin' back to the DART station!"

She smiled brightly, her tone as enthusiastic as a troop leader psyching up a bunch of Girl Scouts for an outing. I stood there as still and expressionless as a dumb china doll, comprehending very little; she might as well have been Klaatu from Mars asking me to join her on the mother ship.

"We're...going to play darts?" I yawned obliviously.

"Oh dear, no! DART is a train station. It's just down the block on Taras Street." I rubbed my eyes and, when I looked at her again, every powdered wrinkle in her pretty brow was furrowed, like she was sizing up if I was high, which I couldn't blame her.

"You'll be stayin' with *me*! I have a lovely home and," she glanced over my shoulder at a room stuffed with luggage and coats, bed linens that looked like the topography of Japan, a radiator festooned with socks and bras, and a night stand littered with candy wrappers and empty Guinness bottles, "I think yeh'll find it more... comfortable."

*

The soft Irish sun was just touching the lace edges of the window curtains when I woke with a start. For a brief moment I had no idea where I was except on the verge of a panic attack, all sweaty, palpitating and taking my breath in gulps. Then there was a tap on the door.

"Bridget Anne? Are you awake, dear? Irish days are very short this time of year and I've made you a lovely breakfast!"

I sucked in a deep breath and held it, feeling the fear drain away at the happy lilt of Great Aunt Molly's accent and the rush of memories that explained why I was in a spotless, white room with watercolors of Irish cottages, a wall festooned at top with plaster appliqués of swags and fruit, and a bed with a pink and white flowered duvet.

"Come in. I'm awake," I muttered, knowing I hardly sounded it.

The door opened tentatively and Aunt Molly peeped around to ask, "Did you sleep well?", then walked in answering her own question. "You must have; you lay down last evening around half six and it's half eight Friday morning!" She was decked out immaculately in a grey woolen skirt and cream sweater, covered with a shamrock patterned apron.

I rubbed my head in disbelief. Friday? Almost a whole day had passed since the plane landed and I had slept through it! The return ticket was for Wednesday. There was so little time. Aunt Molly placed a pink fleece robe at the foot of the bed and said, "Put this on. You can dress after breakfast."

Delicious aromas led me downstairs. I passed an empty formal dining room on my way to sounds of Irish music and scraping spoons, and scents of deliciousness. The kitchen was a cozier arrangement and a small table laden with fresh juice, sausage, potatoes, eggs, pancakes, and more awaited me inside. A crystal pitcher gleamed with an amber liquid that I guessed to be maple syrup. Dewy pats of yellow butter radiated in sunny spokes from the center of a floral plate. A delicate willow basket lined with white linen held several smooth, pale rolls.

"Wow! So much food! You didn't have to fuss!"

"Oh, no fuss, dear. Just about what I usually prepare for m'self and Mr. O'Hora. Yer typical Irish breakfast really."

"Where is Mr. O'Hora?" I'd met him only briefly the night before when I'd hopped off the train, groggy and disoriented, but I recalled a short, amiable, white-haired gent with a turned up nose and cherry round cheeks. It was obvious that my uncle was a leprechaun.

"Your great uncle. Fionan, as I'm sure he'll want you to call him, is anxious to spend more time with yeh but he takes his mornin' walk along the Irish Sea every day this time. We keep very regular habits. He's already eaten but I let you sleep in and waited to join you."

Sleep in? Eight o'clock was sleeping in? At some point during the train ride to Dun Laoghaire and the walk to my aunt and Uncle's home I had contemplated whether, in a moment of weakness, I'd caved too easily into my family's well-meaning intervention. Great Aunt Molly was sweet but I knew that once I got a grip I'd probably regret the impaired decision to fold myself under her watchful wing. *Maybe I should have protested, insisted on staying at the hostel, continued my adventure exactly as planned.* These thoughts floated back full force along with a new kind of discomfort. Still, I tore into the meal and my aunt looked pleased at my delight in the food if not my slightly more casual manners.

"The sausages are delicious," I said tentatively, looking for a way to make conversation with this stranger who was my blood relation.

"We call them bangers here, dear. Put yer napkin in yer lap. I'm glad yeh like them."

My uneasiness stole my words for most of the meal, leaving me with little to iterate but requests to pass condiments and ask about the contents of a bottle labeled "Brown Sauce". Fortunately, Great Aunt Molly's upbeat chattiness of the day before seemed to be her usual modus operandi and she gave me a rundown of family matters, mostly about people I'd never heard of. Then she launched into the story of her life with Mr. O'Hara from the day they'd met at church in Sligo to their move to Dublin to raise a family and his good fortune in the banking business.

"And when Mr. O'Hara retired we stayed on here. We both so love the Irish Sea. We'll all go for a stroll together later on."

Fortified by sleep and food, I decided to make a case for the plans that had originally brought me to Ireland. I quickly swallowed a soft mouthful of eggs to get a word in before Great-Aunt Molly continued again.

"I'm only going to be here a few days, Aunt Molly. I actually came here to..."

"I know why you came here, dear." My aunt wiped her lips delicately and put her own fork down. Her voice was firm and had a slight edge to it. "Your brother Michael told your grandmother what was in the note you left."

Drat, Michael! Since when did he have a confession complex and need to tell Grams everything? I bit my lip and nodded, waiting for the "Are you crazy?". Instead she asked: "How did you think to find her?"

"I dunno. I looked a lot of stuff up on line and found out that the National Library has an amazing geneaology department with records of properties and businesses for hundreds of years. I figured I'd do some research, ask around, see if someone remembered her or her shop." I recalled the ride to the hostel and how daunted I'd felt by the size of the place. "I guess I thought maybe Dublin was a small enough town. I thought it might be easy to...that I could..." Frustration caught the words in my throat. Molly leaned over and gently laid her hand on my arm.

"Bridget, sweet girl. I know yer family is after havin' a lot of trouble, and I know yer heart's in the right place, but surely you don't believe anythin' that's happened is the result of some silly old curse."

Of all the reactions I might have anticipated, directness was not one of them, so all I could do by way of answer was to blurt out the truth in equal bluntness. "The way Dad tells the story, I thought the whole family believed in it." It came out defensive, almost suspicious.

Great Aunt Molly cast her eyes down and drew back, picking up her plate and taking it over to a plastic pail near the small kitchen's sink.

"Oh, there's been talk but..." she wasn't making eye contact and she paused to scrape the plate for a long time, "...that's all it is. Talk. Old folk tales. When bad things happen, people want to make sense of it. And when young people die it's so senseless that..."

She laid the dish in the sink, her back to me, and stopped a moment before turning to the table with a forced little smile.

"It's like Princess Diana. A tragic accident but, o' course, people are still runnin' around screamin' 'conspiracy' because we've got to put a meanin' to the death of one so young and promisin'." I scrutinized her face as she took my plate but she stared down at the few microscopic scraps I'd left as intently as an astronomer studying the craters of the moon and did not meet my eyes.

"So you're saying that the whole story about Maggie was made up after the children died, *after* bad things began to happen?"

"Well, no, not exactly. The thing is..." all the cheer was out of Great Aunt Molly's voice. She looked serious and a little worried. Back at the sink again, she scraped and rinsed so long that her silence disturbed me.

"The Irish are great exaggerators," she offered finally. "I'm sure there are tiny bits and pieces of truth in the story your father told you but," she returned to her chair at the head of the table, "why don't you just tell me what you know."

It had to be nine o'clock. I knew the library would be open by the time I got to town and my resolve to continue with my original plan was only growing. I retold Dad's story in a short and sweet version.

"And so I figured if I could find Maggie, maybe I could make her see what a fix she's gotten us all in and convince her to try to change

126

things."

"And how do you propose to do that?"

I knew exactly what I was going to ask my aunt Maggie if I ever found her but something in Aunt Molly's demeanor made me hold back.

"First things first, Aunt Molly. I have to find her. I'd really like to do what I came here for and spend a day in the library trying to find Maggie's store."

My aunt tried a new tack. "Oooh, such a shame. The Christmas decorations are all out on Grafton Street. I thought we'd spend the day shoppin', havin' lunch at this darlin' place I know called Leon's. Do you like pastries?"

There was a sense of battle lines being drawn and I stood my ground. "Couldn't we do that *after* a visit to the library? They're closed on Mondays and I haven't got much time."

Molly pouted like a spoiled little girl who'd just been told that Santa wasn't leaving her the expensive new dolly she'd requested for Christmas. I didn't like this side of her. She bit her inner lip as if to keep something from spilling out of her mouth and sighed exasperatedly. "I suppose not. Still, I think you're wasting your time, but you have come a long way, after all."

"Thank you, Aunt Molly. If it isn't too much trouble." I caught myself sounding a little sarcastic. My aunt had been kind to me and she really was a sweet old lady who probably didn't need a runaway great-niece she'd never met sticking a nasty cog in the smooth and regular wheel of her little bayside life. Her nephew had just died. She'd been away from home for weeks.

"No trouble at all, really," she replied a bit

coldly.

Cut her a break, Bran.

"I'm really sorry to be so insistent, Aunt Molly. It's just that I went through so much to get here. I just want to do a little research. If I come up all dead ends, we can shop and lunch and walk along the Irish Sea and you won't hear another peep out of me, I promise, but I know I won't feel satisfied until I try."

My great aunt opened her mouth to respond but we were both distracted by the sound of the living room entrance squeaking open on its old hinges.

"Molly, m'love! I'm home. Did I give you enough time?"

I turned to judge at my aunt's reaction to that statement but she had dashed out the kitchen door and was muttering something to Great Uncle Fionan before I could push back the heavy oak chair to get up off the table.

*

The walk to the train station was more memorable with a clear head and a full stomach but the cold wind that bit my face would have offered a cleansing even if I hadn't had twelve hours of sleep. The wild Irish sea roiled alongside the walk that ran parallel to the bay and I could barely keep my eyes off the relentless walls of waves that moved in like dark grey steel beams and bashed into foam against the rocks.

"Boats sailed on this thing?"

Great Aunt Molly laughed. "Still do! The yacht club is just ahead!"

Having never seen a body of water rougher than Lake Hopatcong, New Jersey, I had sudden and new respect for Irish sailors.

My great aunt purchased our tickets from a machine, protesting my offer of payment with a wave of the hand and a curt "Nonsense!" We ran the paper cards through a turnstile, jumped on the next train, and were back in the heart of Temple Bar at Taras Street station in less than twenty minutes.

The street that lined the Liffey River was a little gritty, with hotels and shops that were more downtown than uptown; it felt familiar. But when we turned down Westmoreland towards Trinity College I gradually began to feel the flavor of old Dublin. Some of the buildings took on a classical look and the stores were quaint - pipe shops staffed by grey- haired gentlemen in tweed suits and book stores that promised truly ancient finds. When the stately columns of the Bank of Ireland appeared around a corner behind us, Great Aunt Molly reminded me that it had been established in 1729.

"I don't think I've ever seen a building like that except in art books. Maybe the Metropolitan Museum. America really is a baby country, isn't it?"

"Dublin's been here since the Vikings so, comparatively, yes, my dear. The library we are going to visit was established in 1877. How does that strike you?"

I shook my head. "I always thought of old buildings as something built in the 50's! This is going to be a new experience for me."

We took a left down Nassau Street, passed

some expensive crafts shops, and made a right down Kildare. My pulse raced as the grey stones of the National Library appeared on the left. It was all I could do to keep my jaw from dropping at the sight of the black wrought iron gates set between the stolid stone posts. Above the gate, in a frame of gothic-looking ironwork, were large gold block letters that said "LIBRARY".

"I guess I'm not in Kansas anymore," I muttered, stopping to stare at a plaque on the left that read Leabharlann Náisiúnta na hÉireann. "I'm glad this gate is so obvious. I don't think I could ever learn Gaelic!"

Molly said something in Gaelic.

"Show off!" I joked, then quickly glanced at her face to see if I'd offended her but she was smiling and pointing ahead to the entrance.

The façade of the building was as impressive as the entrance. It was a sort of porch formed by a series of columns in a circular pattern; my great aunt called it a portico. Walking around Dublin with her was teaching me that my architectural vocabulary was pretty limited. Back home the only architectural terms I used were "house", "mall", "office building" or "department store" and words like "brick", "wood", or "siding" sufficed to describe them. Here I was faced with buttresses and pilasters, rotundas, pediments, and coffered ceilings.

We made our way through white wooden doors into a round room ringed with stained glass windows depicting famous writers: Homer, Chaucer, Milton, Vergil and Dante stared from their niches into the center of the room where there were more columns arranged *inside* the building around an intricately detailed mosaic floor of winged gryphons and floral motifs.

"This place is amazing!" I whispered, staring down at my feet at a mosaic banner emblazoned with the word "Sapientia".

"That's Latin for 'wisdom'," informed Molly.

"Wisdom. Because anything and everything you might want to know is contained inside a library, because wisdom is a search for knowledge."

"Sometimes, wisdom is knowing when to stop searching," Molly replied under her breath, hustling towards the desk on the right side of the room and turning on an extra cheerful grin for the curly-haired young man at reception.

"Good day! How can I help you?" Blue eyes and a dimpled smile looked up from the computer.

"My niece is visiting from the United States and she'd like to avail herself of the genealogical services."

"Well, the geneaology department is right up the top of the stairs on the left but you're required to check your bags and coats in the lockers first. Nothing but pencils and paper are allowed inside the building. If you don't find what you want in geneaology, you'll need a ticket to get into the main reading room."

"I have my form filled out here," I said, pulling papers from my tote and proffering the document across the desk. Great Aunt Molly almost got whiplash turning towards me, an expression of surprise replacing her cheer as I continued. "I think what I need are Thom's

Directories. I want to find a store that used to be in Dublin in the 60s."

"Thom's would do the trick for you. But you still might try a visit to genealogy first." As Mr. Curly Hair checked my documents and stamped them, Molly continued to stare at me.

"What? I did my homework! I e mailed the library a couple of times before I came here."

We climbed a short flight of stairs to the locker room where a congenial guard showed us how to establish our own combination in the electronic glass bins. For free. *Not in the states,* I thought as I stashed my things. Aunt Molly took another locker for her belongings, folding her spotless fuchsia cape as carefully as if it were the Shroud of Turin before placing it inside over her trim clutch bag.

We climbed the first flight of stairs past intricately carved marble posts and through the equally decorative oak doors of the geneaology room. It was already filled with patrons and every one of the computer stations was occupied but I didn't mind; I was fairly certain that I wouldn't need them. I thought it would be best to start at the beginning and find out about her business in Dublin. From a few questions I'd posed through the libraries website, I was fairly certain that Thom's was the only directory that was going to help me.

Out of curiosity I lifted the thick, dog-eared folders and worn cloth bound volumes lying about on the desks - records of wills, gravestone inscriptions, property valuations, births, deaths and marriages - but I soon lost patience.

"Do you know the name of Maggie's store

or the street it was located on?" I asked Molly as she thumbed absently through a frayed green volume titled General Alphabetical Index to the Townlands and Towns, Parishes and Baronies of Ireland.

She looked surprised at the question and hesitated a bit before answering.

"Mum didn't like to talk of it much and I didn't have much of a mind to ask. I was a young girl busy with school and friends. All I recall is that she told me it was a confectioners shop."

"A candy store? I thought it was a café."

"A confectioners is a shop that sells sweets and pastries. You can sit and enjoy your cake with a cup of tea in some places. That's the kind of store my sister had."

Just another name for café. Not much by way of new information.

Her tone was forcibly airy but there was something more in her face and I narrowed my eyes as if I could search it out. "And you don't know the name."

Molly looked down at the index again as if it was a riveting novel. "I...I don't recall my mother ever mentioning. As I said, she didn't like to speak of it."

Her demeanor puzzled me. Dad had always told me "Everything happens for a reason" and my hopes upon meeting my Irish aunt were that she had come into my life to help me find her sister, but she seemed to feel that her place was to discourage me entirely, to ward me off and turn me back from my quest.

I closed the yellowed and taped pages of a frayed Townland Index from 1901. "Let's go up to the reading room and look at the Thom's. Maybe it will jog your memory a bit as we leaf through the shop names."

I knew was a long shot. A three thousand, one-hundred-and-twenty- three-mile-long, long shot. Save going door-to-door asking about Maggie like a genealogical Jehovah's Witness, I figured that Thom's was most likely my last chance. If the lengthy registers I was fingering were any indication, it wasn't going to be easy to find an unnamed store owned by one Maggie Connor on an indeterminate street during an inexact year. But it was better than staying in New Jersey doing nothing.

We made our way up a regally curved flight of marble steps and through two more deeply carved doors into the reading room. I had never imagined that a library could make one catch their breath but the room was beyond beautiful. The doors and the panels above them were carved with scrolls, faces, stylized leaves and lion's heads, all framed by flat wooden columns ("pilasters" corrected Molly when I commented on them). Huge, gold, candlestick-shaped lights, ornately wrought and capped with molded-glass shades that resembled flames, were perched above rich wooden partitions. Niches and windows alternated above a border of little, naked, winged angels who danced around the perimeter of the room holding garlands of plaster fruits and flowers. The ceiling that capped this grandeur was half of an oval dome and coffered with rows of panels that gradually changed colors from a deep teal at the base to a light sea foam green at the topmost row, just before a skylight opened up to allow natural light into the space.

All I could offer by way of comment was a long, drawn out "Wow!"

Back on earth, rows of numbered wooden desks stood like soldiers on the parquet floor, each one issued a green glass reading light for their watch over the literary goings on.

"I bet James Joyce must've sat in one of these chairs," I whispered.

"I've often wondered that myself. What famous footsteps am I followin' in this glorious buildin'? It's truly a national treasure."

I showed my paperwork to the gentleman at the desk. "I'd like to see Thom's Directories please."

"Right behind you. Case two."

Directly across the room was a tall case marked with a Roman numeral and filled with red books.

"Unbelievable! Some of these books are from the 1700s!" I felt at once privileged and frightened to touch them.

The books were well within reach once I moved aside an old fashioned wooden step ladder. I pulled one out and held my breath all the way to an empty desk where I placed it down like it was a raw egg.

"Well, here goes." The thick volume fell open to the page that contained its list of features.

"Editorial preface, index, street list, alphabetical list...." I didn't know where to begin. Great Aunt Molly took a seat next to me and stared over my shoulder, arms folded thoughtfully. "Are you sure you have no clue? An area maybe? I have a street map of Dublin, even if I could narrow it down it would help."

Molly sighed, bit her lip, and kept her eyes on the volume. I got the impression that she was avoiding looking at me.

"No, no clue," she answered laconically. I wanted to shake her, to confront her, to accuse her of hiding something, but the composure and grandeur of the reading room was most definitely not the place for one of my temper tantrums. Instead, I sighed loudly and turned to the list of merchants recorded by last name of the owner.

Once again, it was surprising not to find an entire slew of Connors but, unfortunately, none of the few represented stood out as a possible lead. I was fairly sure that no matter what type of establishment my great aunt had owned, it couldn't be referred to as a "chandler" or a "tobacconist". Those pages quickly exhausted, the street listings proved even more daunting. My aunt began to tap her fingers on the desk.

Trying to engage her, I leaned towards her whispering, "What area of town would be most likely to have a coffee shop?" It was almost like asking which street in a US city might be most likely to have a Starbucks on the corner so her reply to my ridiculous question was an appropriate, dismissive little explosion of air between the lips.

The pages of the directories were onion-skin thin and there seemed to be thousands of them but, in spite of this, I doggedly continued to turn them for nearly an hour and a half longer, ignoring Molly's multiplying sighs as I ran my finger down column after column looking for anything that might sound like a café.

Great Aunt Molly began checking her watch with obvious impatience.

"Dear, it's well past lunchtime and I'm truly feeling peckish. Do you think we might call it a day and get something to eat? The library opens at 9:30 am tomorrow. If you've a mind to spend the rest of your stay here, I will come back with you in the morning."

Her offer proved she had picked up on my growing concerns about the futility of the venture. Then, her scout leader demeanor engaging full force she added tantalizingly, "Of course, if your work is done, I would love to take you to see the sights. Have some fun."

A crushing wave of defeat hit me harder than any wave in Dublin Bay as the hopelessness of my blind search finally settled in my gut like a heavyweight punch. Who was I kidding? I had completely underestimated the task at hand. There was no way I was going to locate the long-lost Maggie without a miracle.

Chapter 8 - Tales of the Crypt

After the library debacle, Great Aunt Molly happily became my tour guide. She hustled me out of bed early on Saturday (a task made easy by the huge amount of sleep I had gotten the night before in order to avoid watching television in Gaelic with her and Great Uncle Fionan) and we left before breakfast.

Our first stop was a restaurant called Leon's where our hostess, who introduced herself as Rachel, and our waiter, Henri, seemed to function as living proof of Irish hospitality. The display case by the entrance enticed with the most amazing display of pastries I'd ever seen. Fruit tarts and little mousse cups filled with layers of strawberry cream, giant Sables with raspberry filling, rich brownies, flaky Napoleons, and glazed éclairs, everything done with a flair.

"What is *that*?" I asked Rachel, pointing to a decadent looking double cream puff with a shiny chocolate glaze.

"La Religieuse? It's pâte à chou filled with chocolate crème pâtissière and..."

"It's mine!" I swallowed hard, hoping to avoid drooling in public.

Rachel escorted us to a table in front of a fireplace and Henri arrived moments later with the pastry, now dressed with a tutu of real whipped cream and garnished with an artistic pirouette of raspberry sauce. The confection was so divine that I almost fainted when it danced down my throat. Washing the chocolaty goodness down with equally rich hot cacao seemed like something I deserved to be arrested for.

Great Aunt Molly had tea and a scone, her good humor returning with the color in her cheeks from the warmth of the fireplace.

"This is so good!" I said, wiping a dab of cream from my upper lip.

"Oh, my! Don't you just love this place? I can eat Irish fare at home any time. I always come here when I come to town. I think it's the best restaurant in Dublin. Would you be terribly bored if we came here again?" I nodded firmly in the negative, unable to speak with a mouthful of chocolate yumminess.

Leon's turned out to be one thing that my aunt and I agreed upon completely. The place seemed to release the tension between us. That plus my determination to avoid any further upsets. I'd been so uncomfortable with her in the library that I had decided to drop the subject of Maggie entirely. I felt beaten but I had not wholly conceded the fight to find her; I just determined to keep my thoughts to myself.

After the decadent pastry breakfast, our first stop was Dublin Castle where I got to see lavish Georgian rooms, the Viking foundations of the city, and the remnants of an old moat in the belly of the castle. I loved every minute of it. After a brisk walk back to Leon's for lunch, we went window shopping along Grafton. They had already hung gigantic crystal chandeliers in the middle of the street with neon signs that wished "Nollaig Shona" to all. The Irish days so short, we had time to enjoy the lights before deciding to head home. I thanked Molly as we boarded the train back to Dun Laoghaire.

"I had a great day, Aunt Molly." *Too great*, I thought. There had been moments of forgetting my brothers and father in the states, of forgetting my reason for being in Ireland in the first place. But as soon as the guilt would well up, so would the memory of my failure at the library. I felt powerless. Aside from knocking on the door of every business in town like some lunatic detective, what avenue was left to explore? Great Aunt Molly's expression turned to concern as I let out a sigh that contradicted my statement.

"Would you mind if I called home when we get to the house?"

"Oh, no dear! I'm sure yer family's worried about yeh so far from home, even under my wing. There's a computer in Mr. O'Hora's study upstairs. Would you like to use that to catch up with some friends?"

I felt the sun come through in spite of the grey Irish sky. A computer? I could e mail dad. Even if he couldn't read my messages right away, I knew I'd feel better writing to him.

*

Great Aunt Molly had knocked herself out trying to entertain me on Saturday so there was no way I was going to balk about getting up early to go to mass on Sunday. But even this turned out to be an interesting experience. St. Joseph's Church in Glasthule was much nicer than the square empty spaces I was used to so I was a little perturbed when Molly told me that they were "modernizing" churches all over Ireland to look just like those square boxes back home.

After a brisk stroll back home along the salt-tanged Dun Laoghaire pier, we sat down to a lunch of Irish stew and homemade biscuits, which was pretty much the main event of the day. My aunt was tired from traveling and running all over with me so, when we were finished eating, she left me to my own entertainment with the pc in Great Uncle Fionan's study.

The study was full of Irish memorabilia, travel souvenirs from every part of Ireland, and plaques commemorating my great uncle's years of service at the Irish National Bank. Family photos crowded the top of the desk, and every kind of knick knack imaginable filled a small curio cabinet in one corner. But all I kept looking for was some sign of Maggie.

I started my search for her again on the pc, Googling myself half blind trying to come up with another lead, another angle. Then I signed into my e mail account to write to Farrell. Thanks to Great Aunt Molly's generosity, confessing my crime to him was easier than it might have been. Since she was picking up my tab everywhere and had gotten the hostel to give me a refund, I hadn't tapped into any of Farrell's money. I knew he might not even be aware of the theft yet but I figured it would be much easier to face the music from three thousand miles away where I couldn't actually hear it.

After I sent my apology/explanation on its way, I began writing to Michael. The low Irish sun was already curving down before I wrote my last sentence: "See you day after tomorrow."

An inhaled breath went staccato with

anxiety. Only one more day in Dublin and I'd be going home a failure, my search fruitless.

Unless.

I tiptoed to the doorway. Opening it a crack let in the sound of Irish music from the living room radio. I crept down the ancient stairs along the edges soundlessly. Molly was napping in front of the fireplace, her knitting slumped onto her lap in tangles that rivaled Celtic knots. Fionan was snoring in an armchair across from her, blanketed by the The Irish Times.

On tiny, tiny feet I made my way back up the stairs and to the study and flicked on Great Uncle Fionan's desk light. With as much speed as I could manage without creating either noise or mess, I began to pull out drawers, lift papers, and hunt through shelves. An address book in the desk looked promising but, if it contained Maggie's name it wasn't evident.

Aside from the desk, most everything in the room was in full view so Great Uncle Fionan's study proved much easier and quicker to deplete of hiding places than Farrell's room had been and it wasn't long before I reached another dead end. My letter to Michael still stared at me from the computer screen when I hit the escape button to stop the screen saver of Irish scenery. "See you day after tomorrow." Send.

I bit my lip in frustration. Only one likely place left. And it wasn't in this room.

Now might be a good time to mention that I was getting tired of doing things that made me feel disgusted with myself. My laundry list of infractions was increasing but, after all I'd been through, it would have been a waste not to give it one more shot. Even though I felt shitty, this did not seem like the time to turn over a new leaf.

I padded softly to the center of the hall. The radio was still playing over the occasional soft snore. I took a deep breath and slunk into Great Aunt Molly's room.

Almost as lavish as one of the bedrooms in Dublin Castle, hers was an explosion of pink featuring a wooden four-poster festooned with almost as many ruffles as Barbie's Dream House. A quick glance at the furnishings told me there weren't too many places to hide things and none that I was going to feel comfortable about searching. It's one thing to trash your boyfriend's closet or a desk and another to rummage through an old lady's underwear drawer. But this time I knew exactly what I was looking for and the most likely spot to find it was the nightstand that held a collection of family photos.

I flicked on the lamp. The light coat of dust on the rich mahogany immediately revealed a very thin rectangle where something had been removed.

My aunt had been occupied with my entertainment from the first moment of her return from Aidan's; she hadn't had time to clean the evidence of a quickly stashed photo.

I slid the drawer open with anticipation and turned over a frame lying face down on some tidily folded scarves. It was a faded picture of a much younger Molly and a Fionan with a full head of hair. Between them stood a smiling young woman who bore a strong family resemblance to my great aunt. Maggie? The woman sported an ornate gold comb that held waves of red hair off her left ear, but anyone could wear a comb.

The clincher was a very tiny but noticable dot on her upper lip.

God's kiss, I whispered softly.

Though the threesome were standing in front of a store, there weren't any discernible details - no street sign, the name of the store indecipherably cut off above their heads. But it still filled me with a rush of hope. Molly knew something. Maybe not where her sister was now but where she'd been, something! It was a start. How could I drag it out of her?

Just then there was the sound of footsteps on the stairs.

Perhaps weeks of subterfuge were making me good at it because my reaction was James Bond quick. I placed the photo back down on the scarves, slid the drawer shut, ran over to the door and threw myself on the floor in front of it just as the footfalls stopped on the landing.

"Aunt Molly? Is that you?" I shouted, trying to disguise my guilt by feigning an innocent revelation of my whereabouts.

The door flung open, hitting me square on the forehead.

"Ow! Darn! Now I dropped it again!"

"What are you doing in here?" Molly asked sharply.

"Oh, I'm really sorry, Aunt Molly," I said, pretending to pick something off the rug. "Here it is! Hold on a sec!" I popped the imaginary item into my mouth, swirled it around, ran to the dresser mirror and went through the motions of putting a contact in my eye. "There! I'm SO sorry! I rubbed my eye on the way to my room and my contact popped out. I couldn't find it in the hall so I figured it bounced under the door. You and Great Uncle Fionan were napping...."

"Just leave." She pushed the door wide open, stepped in to own the room, and gestured towards the hall.

"I'm sorry, Aunt Molly."

"Just get out." Her voice was as icy as Dublin Bay in January.

I had one more day to spend with her. The thought of that brief span of time hit me on two levels. First, I didn't feature spending that last day under suspicion with both of us feeling uncomfortable but, more importantly, I realized that one day might not be enough for me to tactfully elicit more information about what I'd discovered. Throwing away the attempted ruse in favor of my usual no-holds-barred bluntness, I wheeled around, deciding to get it over with, clear the air, and let the chips fall where they may.

"You don't believe me, do you?"

"Don't take me for a fool, young lady. I'm sixty-four years old but you may have noticed that I don't wear glasses. I've stared at you from no more than two feet away across Leon's tiny tables and I'd have noticed if you wore contacts." Her lips were pressed together in a pencil line as thin as a crack in ice.

"Okay.   Cards on the table.   I *was* snooping. And I'm sorry I had to go to that length but you can hardly play angel here because I wouldn't have had to snoop if you had told me the truth!"

Molly's eyes flashed sparks that could have

set the rug on fire as she soundly smacked me across the face.

"You cheeky little American brat! What makes you think that you have any right to know the truth? I barely hear from my sister-in-law, Kathleen. I've met your father and some of my American nephews once. Now you come bargin' over to Dublin claimin' kinship with the Irish Connors because our troubles finally found a way into your life!?"

Whoa! Talk about cards on the table. I rubbed my cheek and tried to remember the anger management techniques I'd learned in health class. Deep breath. Count.

"I'm sorry, Aunt Molly, but I didn't even know about your troubles *until* they made their way into my life. And, with all due respect, wouldn't it benefit the Connors on both sides of the Atlantic if I could stop it?"

"Don't make me laugh! If the curse existed, don't you think my sister would have stopped it if she could have? She might have been resentful of all of us, she might have been cold, but she wasn't a monster."

"I understand that. I do. But you must understand why I'm so desperate to find her. How did you feel when your nephews died? How did Aidan feel when he lost his son? Helpless? That's how I felt when I saw my brother, Sean, lying in a hospital bed in a coma, and Brian bruised and bleeding. That's how I felt when I found out my father had a heart attack. They were hurt and in trouble and all I could do was stand by and watch bad things happen. I felt completely powerless. And *I can't stand feeling like* that! I had to do something."

I took another deep breath, stilling my quivering lip. "Don't you see? I know what I did was crazy. I begged, borrowed and stole to get here. I may be feisty but I don't *do* things like that, Aunt Molly! And I'm not usually the sort of person who repays people who've been kind to me by snooping around in their drawers. But I'm also not the type of person who just sits around and lets things happen either. I have to take action or I can't live in my own skin. And now that I've gone through so much to get here, I don't want to go home without any answers, without having at least tried to fix things."

My aunt's face softened a little but she was breathing heavily. "I'm sorry, dear. I'm sorry I hit yeh and I'm sorry that you and your family have had so many tragedies but, most of all, I'm sorry I can't give yeh what you want."

She crossed over to the nightstand and picked up a photo of two small children, one an angel face of around three years old with curly red hair, the other an equally cherubic infant. A stray tear escaped from her eye as she looked down at the picture.

"I remember clearly when Aidan's sweet babies died. I felt just like you do now. Angry, frustrated, and helpless. Mum went searchin' for Maggie but it didn't change a thing. Then, when I married and moved to Dun Laoghaire, I called on my sister in town.

"She was my only sister. There was little love lost between us growing up but I was young and idealistic and thought we could perhaps be friends since she no longer had a cause to be

147

jealous of me or my brothers. And, I admit, I had the same hopes you had. That I might learn something and change things. But more had changed than Maggie's face.

"You know, they say that the opposite of love isn't hate, it's indifference. That's the best name I can give to my sister's attitude. It was like the longer she left Sligo, the more Sligo left her. She was pleasant at first but I think she was just letting me in so she could parade her success in front of me. When I started asking questions she started to avoid me and we lost touch completely after she sold her store. Only God knows where she is now, Brandy. I'm sorry." She smoothed the apron she was wearing, put down the photo and laid her hand upon my shoulder as she sighed.

"Now, I was just after makin' a snack for myself and Mr. O'Hora. If you'll forgive me for slappin' you, I'll forgive you for snoopin' in my room. Will you join us?"

"I'm not very hungry," I replied, "but how about if I come down for a cup of tea?"

Great Aunt Molly grabbed my shoulders and hugged me. "That sounds fine, dear. I am so, so sorry. About everything."

I hugged her back. "Me too, Aunt Molly. Me too."

*

My last day at my aunt's house began like the first as I awoke early to the smells of toast and frying meat. My hunger rushed me through a shower so brief that it made me wish that the Guinness record keepers had been there to time

148

it.

"Ah, Brandy! You're up early!" Molly said, pouring me a cup of tea from a floral china pot. Breakfast today was in the dining room. "And we really don't have to rush today because Great Uncle Fionan has business in town. He's going to drive us in!"

"Yes! I haven't had much time with you girls the past few days. We can talk in the car a bit. Then we'll get together for a farewell dinner at Leon's. Although, I hear yer allergic to pastries," he winked.

"So, where would you like to go on your last day in Dublin?" Molly's Girl Scout leader voice was back full force.

"Honestly, Aunt Molly, I didn't give the sights much thought before I came here." I wanted to mention that the guy at the hostel had suggested the Guinness factory tour but I couldn't picture my aunt's cloche and cape sweeping around a brewery. "We've seen Dublin Castle, the library, and Trinity College. Do you have any ideas?"

Great Aunt Molly beamed. "Actually, I do! You enjoyed our little church so much yesterday, I was hoping you might want to see St. Patrick's Cathedral and Christ Church."

I would have asserted a choice for the Guinness factory then and there but for her description of St. Joseph's as a "little church". It had been the most massive church space I'd ever been in. What could St. Patrick's and Christ Church possibly look like? The Taj Mahal? My curiosity was definitely piqued, but I had my doubts; spending my last day inside churches didn't exactly sound like a thrill. So I opted for a moment of non-committal silence to see which way the wind blew.

"You did like St. Joseph's didn't you?" asked Molly tentatively.

I nodded vigorously, anxious to dispel any doubts about my honesty after last evening. "Oh, yes! It was very impressive!" But, although it was true that I'd been impressed, I was beginning to think I'd overplayed my enthusiasm.

"Well, then we must go! I think you will be pleasantly surprised," chirped my aunt, forking more pancakes onto my plate.

I managed a convincing enough grin through a mouthful of bangers.

*

Great Uncle Fionan turned out to be a pisser. He made jokes all through breakfast and I was sorry I wouldn't have more time to get to know him better. Unfortunately, his driving was equally as crazy as he was.

"Traffic lights in Ireland are strictly fer decorative purposes!" he laughed as he gunned through a main intersection. "Go scriosa cúnna ifrinn do chuid fo-éadaigh!" he yelled at the car that nearly clipped us. Great Aunt Molly giggled.

"What did he say?"

She put her hand delicately over her mouth and laughed some more.

"What?"

"May the hounds of hell destroy your underwear!" translated Great Uncle Fionan with a smile on his face as wide as Connell Street. Los' driving back home was crazy but Great Uncle Fionan really freaked me out. Bad enough everyone was driving on the wrong side of the road. He chattered on enjoyably about Glendalough and other sites in Ireland that he wished I'd had time to see but I was relieved when he dropped us off in front of the grey stone façade of St. Patrick's Cathedral.

Once we made our way inside I had to admit I was pretty satisfied with my aunt's choice. You probably could have fit two or three St. Joseph's inside the massive space. On top of that, the way the windows and arches were designed practically yanked your head back to look up. Every dark niche and alcove contained something fascinating: a cap stone for an ancient well upon which the church was founded, a weathered door that figured in the settlement of a feud between two lords in 1492, statues and plaques commemorating famous Dublin citizens, medieval tiles, ornate tombs and chapels in use since the 1600s, a fabulously carved marble pulpit and spiral staircase. But the most exciting part for me was the choir stalls, rows of rich mahogany benches with thickly carved backs that curliqued upwards into a pinnacle where glittering swords capped with whole headpieces from knights' armor perched like an empty army. Over each of them hung thick, multicolored regiment banners, heavy with dust and time. The light filtered in dimly but and left my imagination to the depiction of the cathedral's glory days when color and gilt must have flashed everywhere.

"Those banners are from the Knights of Saint Patrick during the time of King George III," informed Molly proudly. "Unfortunately, I don't believe anyone's been up there to clean them since then." She sniffed and marched off indignantly to another spot, her spotlessly clean feathers ruffled by the dust of ages.

I caught up with her standing in front of a massive tomb with a marble effigy of the dead man it contained.

"Wow. I can't believe I wanted to go to Guinness Warehouse! Who would think that visiting a church could be so fascinating?" I said absently as I strolled up behind her. I wasn't being sarcastic but Molly raised her eyebrows so high I thought they'd hit the brim of her cloche. "Oh. The desk clerk at the hostel told me about the tour. I didn't *really* want to go."

"Guinness isn't too far from here if yeh want to skip Christ Church. I wouldn't want to keep yeh from the edifyin' experience of going to a brewery." It was clear to me at that moment that my sarcasm was hereditary.

"I didn't mean what I said about the church in a bad way. It really is fascinating and I like it. It's just...I didn't think I was going to like it so *much*, that's all." My mouth seemed to be stuck in permanent "offend" mode. "Look, Aunt Molly, I know it's been a little difficult but I am happy that I came to Ireland, happy I met you and Great Uncle Fionan. And Dublin Castle and this place....they're all about my history too." I took both her hands and held them firmly. "I'm enjoying this, honestly. And, if Christ Church is half as interesting as this place, I wouldn't miss it!"

Great Aunt Molly smiled again. "Half?

Well, it's over a hundred and fifty years older for starters! And it has a crypt in its medieval undercroft that is open to the public. Most interesting!"

It was only with superhuman strength that I forced my face to keep its pleasant expression. I hadn't told my aunt about the banshee. Maybe if I'd played that card from day one she'd have shared her knowledge of Maggie, however useless, but I knew that there was also the chance that I'd have found myself in Dublin's equivalent of an insane asylum. Either way, I stood there wishing I'd gone full disclosure because the *last* place a person who's seen banshees wants to be is in an underground crypt.

*

We had a quick cup of tea and shared a raisin scone at a little place across from Christ Church before we entered the cathedral. Unlike, St. Pat's, it was fairly bright inside, making it easier to see all the beautiful details. And although the cathedral was older, it seemed in better condition, with less of the dust that disturbed Great Aunt Molly. I grew comfortable, cheered even, so that, after walking around gawking at the dramatically lit art and architecture, I didn't feel so fearful about visiting the crypt when we'd had our fill of inspiration.

"I've seen how yeh observe architecture and I know yer going to love this. It's one o' the largest crypts in Britain or Ireland," gushed Molly as we climbed down the white stone steps. "This building was constructed by a Viking king on the foundations of a Viking settlement. Yeh can see evidence of that through a glass in the floor downstairs. The monuments aren't much different from those we've seen upstairs but I think it's amazing to see the foundations of such a great building, don't you? To think that the stones below are holdin' up all this! All supported by natural materials made in a time when men did the work with their hands on scaffolds, not machines and cranes."

I found myself growing just as excited as she was. I was stepping into history, into a time long gone. It was like being in a movie set and a time warp all rolled into one.

The crypt was far tamer that I expected. If the upper stories were well lit, the crypt almost looked like a Christmas display. There were spotlights in the floor and overhead, illuminating most of the potentially scary corners. Two bright ones flashed off the first statues that greeted us, which were of such white marble that they could have been used to create Hollywood dental veneers.

"This isn't so spooky," I mused, walking over to read the inscriptions.

The columns in the room wound around a bit disjointedly. Or maybe I was wound a bit disjointedly. It had been a long week and a long day. I lost my aunt as I zig-zagged around and through the stolid stone supports as if they were Maypoles. Off to one darker corner I noticed a little glass case, the only one in the undercroft. Curiosity aroused, I meandered over for a better look, expecting to see a piece of broken statuary, but the blood left my veins when I realized it was the shriveled, crispy remains of a cat and mouse that had both lost the battle with death in a chase through the pipe organ.

"Heeeee!" The sharp intake of breath was much too loud for the quiet space, amplified by the fact that it was a slow day and my aunt and I had the room all to ourselves. I clapped my hand over my mouth as she called out to see if I was alright.

"I'm fine! Fine, Aunt Molly!"

She began to walk over from the opposite end of the crypt. I could hear the tap, tap of her pumps growing louder as she came closer. When I spied her about thirty feet away, the spots in the arches flickered with a high-pitched little electrical buzz.

"Oooh! What was that?" She paused instinctively.

"A glitch of some sort. Maybe we should go?"

As if to back me up, the lights flickered again with the same piercing hum.

"It *is* getting close to...." she only took a few more steps before all the lights died and we were thrown into a darkness so black it was as if we'd been buried alive.

Great Aunt Molly's tapping came to a complete and sensible halt. "Bridget Anne? Are yeh alright?"

"Yes, I'm right here."

"Don't move."

I had no intention of moving. I couldn't have found my way out of the space with night vision goggles so I figured my main job was to try not to panic and fall over a sword somewhere.

"We should both stay still until the lights come on again."

"Yes, yer right. I was so close to yeh though, I....." Molly's voice trailed off oddly. The sound of current flowing through a shorted connection took up again.

"There's that buzz, Aunt Molly. The lights will probably be on in a minute." A cold wind blew across my cheek and I shivered. "Does it feel cold to you in here without the lights on?"

"Bridget Anne, don't move." My aunt's voice was trembling. The electrical hum was beginning to take on a familiar tone. *Oh, no! Aunt Molly's going to think I'm nuts. I've got to keep it together.*

Icy fingers crawled over my shoulder.

"Aunt Molly? Is that you?"

"I'm right here, Bridget. Are yeh still feeling alright?" Her quivery voice was still across the room but the sound of the whine was growing stronger and louder behind me.

"Just c-c-cold. Very cold."

"Just stay calm, Bridget." Good advice that she wasn't taking herself since her voice shook like a rattle. "Let's say a p-prayer. That will comfort us in the dark."

By now I knew it was the banshee screaming in my ears. Light-headed and freezing, I broke out in a clammy sweat. Molly began to say the Lord's Prayer in a loud voice, as if to drown out the keening of the banshee she could not hear.

"Our Father, who art in heaven...." The wailing grew along with Molly's tone.

"....hallowed be thy name. Why don't you

156

join me, Bridget."

"Thy kingdom come. Thy will be done...."
We chorused in unison but it wasn't enough to drown out the banshee's screams. I pressed my hands against my ears and shouted the words.

"...on earth as it is in heaven."

My voice quivered in my throat while my brain screamed my real prayer: *Please, God! Just make the lights come back on!*

"Give us this day, our daily bread."

The banshee began calling my name.

"Briiiiiiiiiiiiiiiiiiiiidgeeeeeeeeeee...."

As if it wasn't dark enough, I pulled my head down to my chest. I did not want to see that face. My eyes closed, my hands smashed over my ears, my forearms pressed over my eyes, I tried to block out every sensation but the sound of my own voice praying loudly.

".... AND FORGIVE US OUR TRESPASSES."

Still I heard her.

"Briiiiiiiiiiiiiiiiiiiiiiiiiidddgeeeeeeeeeee...."

"...AS WE FORGIVE THOSE WHO TRESPASS AGAINST US..."

The otherworldly wind wrapped around me in the blackness like a shroud. Tears began to fall in stinging drops down my arms; I bent over, rolling myself into a tighter ball.

"AND LEAD US NOT INTO TEMPTATION...."

My voice rose against the flood of sounds like a seawall holding back the unrelenting pounding of waves

"....BUT DELIVER US FROM EVIL!"

Something had taken a hold of me. The

banshee's cold hand was no longer on my shoulder but she was shaking me, calling me. I lifted my chin and felt the sensation of light on the lids of my eyes. I opened them to see Great Aunt Molly's face in front of me, shouting my name as if I were deaf.

"Bridget Anne, snap out of it!"

How was I going to explain this? What story could I possibly concoct to stop my aunt from thinking her niece was certifiable?

"Why did yeh cover yer ears? Did yeh...did yeh hear somethin' when the lights went out?" she asked, the sound of fear in her voice much more exaggerated than someone who had to stand in the dark a few moments.

"Did...did you?" I already looked like a nut case, I didn't want to admit to anything.

"I...I thought.... I saw somethin'. On yer shoulder. Did yeh...did yeh feel anythin' on yer shoulder?"

I gasped. "You *saw* her!" My aunt's mouth opened wide. "The banshee! You saw her!"

A chill ran from Molly and through me as if, together, we were two currents of fear that had completed a circuit.

"Oh! Oh, my! I...I need to sit down. Let's get upstairs. We need to talk."

*

Dad was right. Everything does happen for a reason. That afternoon at Christ Church proved to be my reason for coming to Dublin.

My aunt was a spry old gal for her age but

158

she could have done an aerobics instructor proud as she flew up the steps to the main floor. I raced right next to her and it was a toss-up as to who moved faster. But by the time we found a seat in one of the pews she was already in denial.

"Maybe I do need glasses after all," she whispered. "I thought I saw..." She stopped. Thought a moment. Shook her head. "It...oh, yeh'll think I'm a mad old bird!"

"Believe me, Aunt Molly, I won't. I've seen her several times."

"A...a white woman. With these horrible red eyes! She had her hand on yer shoulder in the dark."

I nodded. "I felt her hand."

"And she started wailin'."

Another nod.

"And you say you've seen her before?"

"Yes. The first time was the night that Cousin Aidan died." I relayed the story of the events at the club, the visits from both banshees, Halloween night, and the sighting in the airplane. I even told her about the way I had hoped to stop the curse. It didn't matter anymore.

"And so I thought I could convince her to cut one last bargain with the banshee and free us all. But I've failed. And now my brothers are going to die." The tears felt like acid on my cheeks. "And more."

With both of us facing the altar it was difficult to gauge my aunt's reaction, but I no longer cared. I was leaving the next day and it didn't matter if she thought I was crazy.

"So, there you have it. Maybe now you can understand why I believe in the curse and exactly how desperate I was to stop it."

Great Aunt Molly didn't reply. From the corner of my eye I could see her unsnapping her clutch bag and, when I finally turned my head, she was dabbing her eyes with a tissue.

"I'm so sorry. I didn't realize. I always thought we Connor's were an unlucky lot but it always terrified me to think of the curse. But, now I can't deny it. Not after today...." Her voice trailed off and she glanced at her watch. "It's time to get on our way to meet Mr. O'Hora for dinner but we need to speak in private when we get home. I have something for yeh at the house that might help yeh and the rest of the boys back in the states."

*

As much as I loved Leon's, I was anxious for my talk with Great Aunt Molly and wanted to skip dessert. Fortunately or unfortunately, depending on how you look at it, my uncle was as much a fan of pastries as I was and had his dessert picked out before the appetizer. In spite of the delay, my anxiety did not prevent me from savoring my last, thick, creamy, chocolate La Religieuse.

"Do you think you'll be visiting us again, Bridget?" Fionan said congenially as he stirred his Café Mocha.

"I would love to. Visiting all the medieval sites and the cathedrals has given me an idea. I've always had trouble deciding whether to major in English or art when I get to college. Now I think I'm going to explore art history or architecture. I think I'd like to come back here and study someday. This country is so fascinating."

"That it is! And you haven't even had any truck with the Little People yet! Now *there's* some fascinating tales! Kelpies and fairies. Tales of leprechauns and boggarts. I know a great tale of the Black Hounds on the heaths. Do you like scary stories?"

Aunt Molly raised her eyebrows and cast me a knowing glance.

"This young lady has a flight to catch, tomorrow morning, Mr. O'Hora. Can't be keepin' her up with those sorts of stories." She patted my hand soothingly. "I think Bridget Anne would prefer a little lighter conversation tonight. Why don't you tell her one of your jokes?"

*

I was rearranging the junk in my tiny suitcase to fit the few souvenirs I had picked up. It was mostly maps and flyers that I had gotten for free but Molly had also given me a really nice, bumpy woolen scarf from Donegal and one of her bulky Irish sweaters that I'd admired. Everything fit fine into the luggage....if I left half of my own clothing in Ireland. I was pulling the sweater out for the third time when Great Aunt Molly knocked and entered, dressed in her fleecy pink robe and woolen slippers, carrying a piece of paper in her hand.

"Almost done, dear?" she asked, comfortably plopping down on the edge of the bed next to my tote.

"Yes. All done. I'm going to wear the sweater and scarf you gave me tomorrow."

"Oh, that's lovely. I'm so glad you like them." She patted the empty space next to her. "Sit down, Bridget. I have somethin' to show yeh."

Reaching into her pocket, she pulled out a pair of reading glasses.

"Um...just an observation here, Aunt Molly, not a confrontation, but...um... didn't you tell me that you had perfect eyesight." I was basically calling my great aunt a liar but there was a big smile on my face. Dad had always told me you could say just about anything to a person with a smile on your face.

"Caught me!" she chuckled. "I'm just a sharp ol' gal. Called yer bluff last night, didn't I?"

I shook my head in amusement. "Touché, Aunt Molly! You fooled me too. I guess I deserved that anyway."

"No. Not really, Bridget." She smoothed a fold of pink fleece down her thigh and grew serious. "When I first heard about yeh comin' here to find Maggie I have to admit I was indignant. I felt that her whereabouts or her curse were none of yer business. When yer grandfather, Peter, married Kathleen and they moved to the states to avoid the fate of Aidan's boys, I felt quite abandoned. I'd already lost a sister and two nephews. Peter's leavin' lost me a brother and a good friend.

"After Mr. O'Hora and I married, we visited the states when your father and Uncle Patrick were just babes. But, as good as Mr. O'Hora did for himself, it was too much to go draggin' our brood to the US once our own babes came.

"And, the resentin' part was there too in another way. It seemed to me that Peter and Kathleen deserted Ireland like rats leavin' a sinkin' ship, leavin' us to our sorrow and burden. And later on, when their brood came, I knew that Peter couldn't afford a trip to Ireland to see me an' mine. But there was this part o' me that knew that all the gold in the world wouldn't have mattered. The real matter was that they were afraid o' the curse.

"So, I suppose I thought it was brassy of yeh askin' for my help when we'd gotten no help here from you and yours. And I still wasn't convinced that it was anything but bad luck." She began to open the envelope in her hand. "Until this afternoon."

Molly placed the letter in her lap and put on her glasses carefully, then she dug into another pocket. Taking out a pen and paper from the folds of her fleece, she handed them to me saying, "Here. Take these."

She arranged her robe and settled herself in a manner that reminded me of Dad when he went into his story telling mode.

"Now I have to be after tellin' yeh that I have heard the banshee a time or two m'self what with all the deaths this family has suffered. I always tried to pass it off to m'self as distant train whistles or screechin' traffic. But...today was no mistaking what I heard. And, in spite of these reading glasses, I see clear as a bell far away and, when I saw that white spectre touchin' yeh today, I like to've died of fright on the spot. I knew then and there that the curse was real, that the troubles of the Irish Connors had crossed the Atlantic, and I felt fear for yeh and yer brothers. Though I've never met them, they're kin just as well, and it seems to me now that my sister is responsible for their pain just as sure as she was for the evil that took Aidan's boys. I don't have to know yer brothers to want to do the right thing. And...," she picked up the paper and shook it emphatically as she continued, "here is something that makes me believe even more that the Lord is workin' for good in all o' this to put a stop to the evil. This is the last known address of my sister Maggie..."

I felt my heart leap as she ended with, "...in the United States."

Chapter 9 - Other Plans

The plane took off uneventfully but I was still excited. Great Aunt Maggie's address was on a small slip of paper in my luggage. And in my purse. And stuffed in my bra. I wasn't taking any chances.

I rolled the new bits of her story over and over in my head.

After Dublin, Maggie had moved to London and opened up a shop called The Painted Pony, named after some song lyrics she loved. Great Aunt Molly said one of the lines was: "We're captive on the carousel of time." That kind of made me shudder. Most people would think only of the perks of forever beautiful but, like any vampire tale will tell you, there is a definite down side to immortality.

Molly guessed her sister moved around a lot because, every few years, Maggie would send a note or a card from a different location. "Perhaps," Molly sighed, "she believed in the adage 'The best revenge is living well' because I always seemed to get a note from her when she was doing particularly well. She had a beautiful shop in Paris for quite some time."

Great Aunt Molly had lost touch with her for several years and then, just this past September, she had received a letter. Maggie had managed to save enough money to move to the states and was running a successful tea shop in, of all places, Philadelphia. Practically in my back yard. The timing bothered me. I couldn't figure out if she'd brought the banshee with her to the states or if the wraith had followed Aidan Jr. It wouldn't have made a difference either way to my brothers but, what bothered me was that it might have made a difference to Aidan Jr. I tried not to think about it too much.

I was still awake when the plane landed in New York. I made my way through customs in record time with my little carry-on suitcase, anxious to get home but not too excited about another shuttle and a butt-busting ride on the train. In the arrivals area, limo drivers held signs and family members kissed. I was feeling a little envious of everyone on the receiving end of either of these benefits when....

"Ooof!" I thought someone slammed a suitcase into me until the suitcase grew arms that folded around my back and I found myself buried face down on Michael's chest.

"Brandy! Are you okay?"

"Noogies you crazy nut! Don't ever do anything like that to me again!" Dylan was there too, rubbing his knuckles on my scalp.

"How's dad? How are Sean and Patrick?"

"Dad's stable. He's coming home in a few days. Sean is...no worse; the docs are hopeful. Patrick is still knitting up."

Vague, vague, and vague.

"Pat's got an infection," blurted Dylan.

"An infection? What kind of infection?"

"Shut up, D! He's fine, Bran. Just a little cellulitus."

"What the hell is that?"

"Some kind of infection," Michael replied. I wanted to say something sarcastic like, *Oh, that explains everything*, but I was too happy to see my brothers to start busting them right off.

"Never mind anyway. Everyone's okay, considering. We've been more worried about you the past couple of days."

"I'm sorry, guys. We all had enough on our plates. I feel really bad about that. Especially for worrying dad."

"We never told him where you were."

"So, how'd you manage to hide a missing daughter for a whole week?

"It was my idea," said Dylan proudly.

"Dad knew you'd cut classes...."

"Ol' Hootie saw to that I bet."

"You got it. Anyway, after I read the note I was freaked. I had to tell Dylan where you were just to stop him from asking about you every five freakin' minutes..."

"And when he told me you went to Ireland I told him to tell Dad we'd found you home in bed with the flu! We said you threw your guts up all over the front steps of the school and never even made it inside and that you were in bed with a hundred and three degree fever and couldn't come to the hospital to see him! Brilliant, no?"

"Very brilliant." I gave Dylan another quick hug around the shoulders. "God! I'm so damn glad to be home. I'm also glad to be able to say damn; I had to watch my mouth in front of Great Aunt Molly!"

"Speaking of...how did it go with her?"

"Let's get out of this place and I'll tell you all about it in the car."

Michael scooped my suitcase up like it was a five pound bag of sugar and we made our way to the parking lot. I was glad to be wearing the sweater and scarf my aunt gave me; New York was colder than Ireland.

On the way home I told my brothers what had happened during my trip. Mostly. Even though I'd mentioned hunting for Maggie in my letter to Dad, I didn't want to get anyone's hopes up.

Nah. That's wasn't it.

I didn't want them to try to stop me from hunting her on home turf.

*

My brothers almost had to pry me out of bed with a crowbar the next morning, but there was no way Michael was letting me miss another day of school. He and Dylan took turns pounding on my door relentlessly while they took their respective showers.

"C'mon, Bran! Michael says he isn't leaving without you. I know *you* don't care if we're late but if I get detention I'll miss band practice and Mr. DiGioia will have a fit."

I turned over and groaned. Jet lag on the home front felt a little less severe but I wanted to spend the day at St. Clare's with Dad, not at school facing Farrell.

"Alright! I'm getting up!" With reluctance I pulled on a black turtle neck and jeans and ran a hand through my short, burgundy crop of hair. Zero makeup. The fashion statement I was hoping to convey was "inconspicuous". It had been a rough week and I wasn't in the mood for attention or questions. My brothers were the only ones who knew what I'd done. And maybe

Farrell if he'd read my e mail.   I'd practically begged him for secrecy but I couldn't have blamed him if he was pissed off and had broken into the principal's office to reprogram the LED message sign in the hallway to read: "My ex-girlfriend Brandy is a thief and a kook. See Dirk Farrell for details."   I had no idea what anyone else at school knew and I winced when I thought about the counselors and psych evaluations that Celeste had gone through after one measly night in White Castle.   They'd be all over a week in Dublin.

"Want some?" Michael shook a box of cereal at me as I entered the kitchen. "You gotta hurry up and eat though cuz...."

"I'm not hungry. Let's get goin'," I replied, fibbing.   There was a cavern in my stomach as deep as the Mariana Trench, but if we got to school early I knew I'd miss seeing, well, mostly everybody. And that was just the way I wanted it.

Mike dropped me and Dylan off together in front of the school and I broke a land speed record for getting to my locker, stashing my things, and running into Crabface's class with my head tucked into my chest behind my notebook. I slumped into a seat in the back of the room as low as I could possibly go without my ass falling on the floor but didn't get ten seconds worth of peace before Crabface walked into the room. I put my head down on my arms, feigning sleep.

"Are you still feeling ill, Bridget?" Crabface called "I can give you a pass to the nurse. You can't keep your head down like that in class, you know."

"I'm fine, Mrs. Pierce."

169

"Too bad you had to be sick over the holidays. I just hate when that happens but it always seems to be the way, doesn't it?" Crabface chattered mindlessly as she fussed with papers on her desk. I was glad when the class started to fill up, pretending to be reaaaalllly engrossed in a book until the first bell rang so no one bothered me.

Second and third period went by just as uneventfully. There was a big advantage to being outside of the general high school social scene. I managed to duck and cover until lunchtime but, as I was rounding the corner to the cafeteria, I spied Farrell coming down the hall from the opposite direction. Unfortunately, he also saw me.

"Brandy!" He quickened his pace like he was charging after a purse snatcher, which I was, sort of.

I did not want a big scene in the halls so I opened my mouth and shouted preemptively. "I was going to call you after school. Please, Farrell, I don't want to have a..."

FOOM! Farrell threw his arms around me and grabbed me in the biggest bear hug since my brother Sean had cracked one of my ribs when I was seven.

"Christ, Bran! I was so worried when I got your e mail!"

"You....you're not pissed?

"Oh, yeah. I'm pissed as hell but...with your brothers being laid up and all, I get what you did. And I still care about you. When are you going to start believing that?"

"Well, I have your money at home...."

"And I've got your cell phone." He started to look for it in his pack. "Listen, do you want to meet at the diner after school?"

"Nah. I gotta go see my dad; he's in the hospital and...."

"What? Why? I'm sorry, Bran, I didn't know! What happened?"

"I'll call you when I get home. If my brothers are out, you can come to my place for awhile tonight...."

"I thought we were hanging out tonight?" Long airbrushed nails slid through the crook of Farrell's arm, followed by a dress code violation of an outfit if I ever saw one. It was Lisa DeLotto; she was either selling fruit for a fundraiser or her own melons were on display, decked out in a low-cut purple top that looked as if she'd tugged the neckline down beyond the capacity of the spandex to retain its shape. "You were supposed to help me with my Bio homework tonight, baby, remember?"

I felt my face turn red with anger. Why did I always believe the best of Farrell only to have him prove the worst?

I turned on my heels and headed down the hall calling "I'll mail you a check!" over my shoulder as the bell rang.

"Bran! Wait! Hold up!"

"Leave my cell in my locker. You have the combo," I shouted as I slid into a crowd of kids rushing for the cafeteria line.

*

I couldn't bear waiting home for Mike to

pick me up after work so I texted him a fib about getting a ride (*Oh my God! This is getting to be a habit now! I'm going to rot in hell if I keep this up!*) and walked to St. Clare's after school in the biting cold. Even Great Aunt Molly's scarf couldn't keep the wind from stealing my breath; my dad's cold room felt like a furnace by comparison when I entered.

"There's my girl!" he smiled.

I threw my arms around him awkwardly. It's never easy to hug someone in a hospital bed.

"You look great, Dad!" I said, fibbing *again* and choking back tears.

"And you don't look too bad yourself for someone who's had the flu for almost a week. Are you sure you're okay? Your eyes look red."

"Just the cold outside, that's all. It made them tear."

"You should have gone straight home after school and waited for Michael or Brian. It's a long way to walk in this weather, even if you're healthy."

"I got a ride. This is just from the parking lot," another fib. "Don't worry about me. How are you? I'm so sorry I couldn't have been here, Dad."

"Never mind. I'm fine. It was a very mild heart attack. It's actually a good thing. Served as a warning. I've known for a long time that I have some habits to change. A little change in diet, some exercise, I'll be better than ever."

"How is your heart attack mild if you've been here a week?"

"Something with my blood tests. It's nothing. I'll be home tomorrow and I'll see

Doctor Randazzo on Monday for a follow up. Piece of cake." He waved off my question but I was anything but reassured.

After we chatted a bit, I shared a typically yukky hospital dinner with him and then went off to see my brothers.

First I went to Sean's room. It broke my heart to see how thin my formerly strapping brother was getting. I knew if I stayed I'd get too upset to keep it together for Patrick so I patted Sean's hand, kissed him on the forehead, whispered, "Get well soon, champ", and walked out with a lump in my throat the size of a baseball.

A few minutes later I arrived at Patrick's room, accidentally barging in on a nurse who was changing the dressing on his wounds. When I saw his leg, I almost threw up the lame chicken parm I'd just picked at in Dad's room. His calf was as red as the inside of a blood orange and covered with huge, misshapen blisters. It looked like something you would see on the National Geographic channel about some isolated jungle tribe that had no medical facilities.

"Just step outside until I'm finished," scolded the nurse.

Gladly! I thought, clutching my stomach. Three minutes later, when she bustled crisply out of the room, I rushed into the bathroom and threw up, playing it off as a remnant of the flu I'd supposedly just gotten over.

"You sure you're okay, Bran?"

"I'm sure I'm not contagious. So, never mind about how I'm feeling. Tell me about your leg."

"It's just an inflammation of the skin. An infection of some kind. They did a culture this morning but the doc says it's no big deal."

No big deal? Dad said he was "fine". Sean looked like a ghost. Patrick's leg looked like it had a flesh eating disease and everything was "no big deal". Everyone was acting brave but we were all falling apart.

When I left Patrick's room I made my way to the public rest room, closed the door, sat on the john, and cried for a good ten minutes,

*

Sometimes I feel like my life is an iPod stuck on permanent shuffle. All I wanted to do was get through the week. Catch up on school work. Get things settled with my family. And find a way to get to Philly on Saturday. But, as John Lennon once said: "Life it what happens while you're busy making other plans."

It was seven-thirty by the time Michael and I got home from hospital visits and a late, quick supper together at the diner. I pulled off my gloves and scarf, willing my feet to keep moving towards my room before collapsing on the bed and turning on the TV. It was a crappy night for programs and I was starting to nod off from exhaustion and boredom when Brian rapped on my door.

"Hey, Bran! Some little bitch named Lisa DeLotto left about twelve nasty messages on voicemail calling you out! What the hell is that all about?"

Just then the house phone rang and I

bolted out of my room and sprinted across the kitchen to get it before Brian could.

"Hello?"

"Bitch? Thachoo finally? You afraid of me, bitch?"

"It's for me, Brian! It's Celeste! I'll talk to you about those other calls when I'm done." I took my hand off the mouthpiece. "Lisa, listen to me and listen to me good. ONE...if you want that shithead, Dork Farrell, you are welcome to him. TWO... my family is having a lot of problems..."

"Oh, you got problems, aight! Your brothers are sick and you got no one to do your fightin' for you!"

"I fight my own battles, Lisa, but I have no fight with you. If you want Farrell, you can have him..."

"You afraid of me? I'm callin' you out bitch!"

"Jesus Christ, Lisa, I'm the one who should be calling *you* out! Farrell and I were back together...."

"You two broke up and he was my man...."

"From what I hear, you screwed him once and he wasn't even interested in seconds..."

"Yeah, bitch, because all of a sudden you want Farrell again and he goes runnin' back to you."

"That's bullshit. We were broken up for over a month. He had plenty of time to screw you more than once if he was interested."

"You still had your claws in him. My girls saw you two at the diner, you jealous little, flat-chested, mosquito-titty, band ho!"

I didn't want to cause anymore trouble but

I knew DeLotto's type. This could never be even a vaguely reasonable conversation and my terrible, terrible temper was much better at dealing with things physically than verbally when the chips were down. Plus, I couldn't have her calling my house at all hours. I had to settle this once and for all.

"Fine, bitch. Where do you want to meet?"

"I'm in front of *La Panateria* on Blackwell, bitch! You want to meet me or should I start to walk to your place?"

"I'll be there in ten minutes."

I pulled out the tiny gold hoops I was wearing. Lisa fought dirty; she'd yank out anything she could grab to draw blood. Then I threw on sweats both for a warm walk and freedom of movement when I finally beat the shit out of her. I crept down the hall and snuck out the front door.

I worked up a nice, adrenalin rush on my way to *La Panateria*. By the time I saw Lisa and two of her friends in front of the bakery, I felt as if I could take all three of them on. But I wasn't stupid. One of her friends was about my size; one was built like the edifice of a small building. Ten feet away from her I shouted:

"Gloves off, DeLotto! Fair fight or nothin'."

Lisa hesitated a minute before pulling off a pair of purple knit gloves. They looked a little leaden when she handed them to one of the thuglettes and I wished I had back up. No one to help me fight, just someone to keep an eye on her two BFFs so they didn't gang up on me.

"And if your two friends get into it, there's

176

plenty of witnesses inside to see how chicken you are to fight me one-on-one!"

"No problem, you ugly bitch. I'm gonna' mess you up! I don't need no help."

The next minute Lisa and I were on the ground tangled like spaghetti at an Italian household on Sunday. My rock band crop gave her very little hair to pull, but I had a really good grip on her bleached locks for a moment. Unfortunately for Lisa, it was just the warm up. With five brothers, I did not fight like a girl. I twisted my legs around hers in a wrestling hold I learned from Sean, plowed my fist into her face, and it was over in three minutes. I scrambled up, on my guard, and as a parting shot, lifted my shirt up to just a second to flash her.

"And I'm *not* flat-chested, you little tramp! I just don't go shoving my tits in everyone's face at school!"

Lisa was hopping around screaming, her nose bleeding all over the sidewalk. The smaller thuglette put her arm around her shoulder and started cursing at me in Spanish while "the wall" came at me in a blur. But before she could get in a good sucker punch, I felt a hand pulling on my hoodie behind me, and the two of us flew apart.

"Break it up! You don't have any problems with this one, do you, Bran'?" It was Michael. He had me by my sweatshirt and the edifice by the shoulder of her jacket.

"No. I don't even know who she is."

For a few seconds we both hung from Michael's arms, swinging like two feisty rag dolls. Then Michael shoved her aside into the still bleeding Lisa and the other thuglette, and planted himself between us.

"Now, as I see it, this fight is over. As I see it, Brandy won and that settles whatever the hell you were arguing about. Now, get the hell home. All of you! Before I forget you're girls!"

Faced with my brothers's anger and biceps, the three of them ducked into *La Panateria*. Michael turned around, pushing me gently ahead of him.

"Did you follow me?" I asked without meeting his eyes.

"Brian listened in on your conversation so I knew where you were headed."

"Are you mad at me?"

"You won, didn't you? Why should I be mad?"

I looked at him. He had the stupidest grin on his face. I smiled back.

"Sucks, though," I said, hanging my head and digging my hands deeper into my hoodie pouch.

"Sucks? Why?"

"Because I don't know if Lisa has friends in that place and they make the best Cuban sandwiches in the whole town!"

*

Celeste rushed up to me and blocked my way into the main entrance of school the next morning.

"Move it! Move it! Move it!" She said, pushing me back through the door and down the front steps.

"What the hell! I'm going to be..."

"Alexis Mendoza and Latricia Taylor are looking for you and they're..."

"Who? I don't..."

"DeLotto's friends. You broke her nose last night. They're going to gang up on you."

"And I'm supposed to...what? Drop out of school? Move out of town?" I shoved past Celeste with determination. "This is such bullshit! Where the hell is Farrell?"

I knew the answer to that question and went straight to his Bio class. He always hung out in front of the door til the last possible minute. But this time he was nowhere to be seen. As I headed towards his locker, I spied him running in my direction.

"Farrell! Could you please call off your dog? And I do mean dog!"

"Brandy! I was looking for you..."

"Oh, I bet you were. Here!" I pulled an envelope with a wad of bills from the side pocket of my pack. "Here's your money. Now tell Lisa and her gangsta bitches that you and I've got no more business left between..."

He grabbed my arm and started to drag me down the hall in the opposite direction.

"Let go of me!"

"Brandy! Shut up! They'll hear you!"

"What the hell are you talking about?"

"Latricia and Alexis. Lisa's friends. They're after you..."

"I know all about it. I don't give a shit!"

"It's two of them against one. Maybe three, considering Latricia's size. Don't be an idiot, Bran!"

"Where're we going? Why should you give

a shit if your girlfriend's buddies are after me?"

"My..? My girlfriend? Oh, for crissakes, Bran..."

He dragged me down a little side hall behind the auditorium, opened the door, and pulled me back stage behind the backdrop. "I've got nothing to do with Lisa DeLotto..."

"Right. I saw her scrunchie in your bathroom..."

"Bran... Oh, shit, really, Bran? After that one time I didn't want anything to do with her. I told you that. It was a big mistake but she keeps glommin' onto me like peanut butter. They guys all call her the Klingon because she hangs on me so much."

"That's not what I heard them call her..."

Farrell rolled his eyes, looking embarrassed. "I swear to you, Bran. I keep trying to avoid her..."

"What about helping her with her Bio homework? That's avoiding her?"

"That was bullshit. She asked me to help her and I told her I was busy but she kept bugging me about it."

"You're not hanging with her?"

"No! I swear. But she's...she's nuts. And her two friends are just as bad and they're running around the school talking all kinds of crap."

"Yeah. Just what I need."

"If you'd given me a chance to explain yesterday..."

"That wouldn't have stopped Lisa."

"Probably not but maybe it could've been handled differently. Anyway, let's go see Mr.

Zullo."

"The drug counselor?"

"He does mediation too. Maybe he can..."

It was too late. The backstage door opened behind us and the unmistakable silhouettes of Lisa's thuglettes were backlit in the doorway, promising more drama than the stage had seen in a long time. The big one barreled towards us but Farrell jumped right in her path.

"BACK OFF, LATRICIA! Do you hear me? Lisa is messed up! She is not my girlfriend and she has no right to tell me who to see or to mess with Brandy!"

"It's not about you, asshole! She broke Lisa's nose last night!"

"It was a fair fight!" I stood my ground near the curtain. "Sorry, about her nose but she shouldn't have stuck it in my business in the first place!"

The Wall advanced, shoving Farrell aside like he was made of paper.

"You go, Latricia!" Alexis egged her friend on.

I never run from a fight but I reconsidered this paradigm as I sized up Latricia again. I'm 5'4" tall. She had to be 5'10". Across. Any action between us could never be anywhere in the vicinity of fair.

"Your brother isn't here to protect you now!" she goaded. I could tell from her tone that this was personal. She was probably pissed because Mike had stopped her from getting her punches in.

I don't run, but I do back up. I brushed aside the canvas backdrop, and pulled it between

181

us to buy some time. Maybe a teacher was in the auditorium and would stop us before she had a chance to land me in St. Clare's next to my brothers.

The front curtains were open and I walked towards them. Okay, quickly. The place looked empty. I got about three feet from the edge when Latricia tackled me from behind and sent me flying off the stage.

*

"I don't know if I can take much more of this, Bran." Michael came back to my bedside in the emergency room with something like his ninth cup of coffee.

"I'm fine! It's just a couple of fractured ribs. One of them is the same rib Sean cracked on me when we were kids so it doesn't even count! It was weak! They didn't even tape me up."

"The doc said they don't do that anymore but you still have to take it easy. And I mean it."

I folded my arms and sighed. "Can we go home now?"

"Yeah, yeah. I'll take your pack."

"It's not that heavy and I'm not an invalid."

"You're not supposed to lift anything for a month."

I grabbed the pack and dropped it in about two seconds. The pain in my right side was all the advice I needed.

"What part of take it easy didn't you understand? The doctor said it's going to be at least six weeks until you're a hundred percent."

Crap. Just what I needed.

"Can we go up and see the boys before we leave?"

"I'm getting you home. You need to get to bed and rest up. Moving around is not a good idea right now."

"But, I want to see..."

Michael glanced at his watch. "No! I'm supposed to be picking Dad up in an hour for release and I've got to get your ass home before that. And since you don't have any visible damage, I think we should try to keep this little incident under wraps. The less Dad knows, the better."

*

I turned on my phone as soon as Mike's car door slammed. Two texts and a voicemail. The texts were from Farrell asking me how I was. Celeste's message was a long one

"That bitch!"

"What's up?"

"Celeste says that Latricia told them she had nothing to do with my fall! She's telling everybody Farrell and I were trying to have sex backstage and I'm covering up for falling off by blaming her! Damn! I can't believe I let that sumo wrestler catch me so off guard."

"Don't worry about it, Bran. I talked to Principal Helmsley. He said there was some little freshman hiding out in the back of the auditorium cutting. They asked him about what went on and he ratted Latricia out when they told him you were in the hospital. You know Helmsley. He probably grilled the kid like CSI and told him he'd be punished as an accessory if he didn't come clean. The lying bitch is gonna be suspended for a month."

"You're kidding, right?"

"No, I'm not kidding, she got sus..."

"I mean, you knew this and you waited until *now* to tell me?"

Michael shot me a dark look. "Cut me a break, Bran! First Sean and Patrick, then Dad. Now I get a call to come fetch your ass from St. Clare's. It's getting so I'm on a first name basis with every freakin' nurse in the hospital. I've got a lot on my mind. Good thing my boss is such a nice guy or I'd be driving to the hospital from the frikkin' unemployment line."

I felt like an idiot. All I could manage was a weak: "Sorry."

"Cripe, Bran," Michael said, anxiously rubbing his hand against his cheek, "what the hell is next?"

I knew the answer to the question but I felt bad about it and kept my mouth shut.

Chapter 10 - Family Matters

After Dublin, a trip to Pennsylvania was hardly going to be epic. But with no money, no car, and three cracked ribs, it was definitely going to be a challenge.

I had to be very careful about asking anyone for help. After my Ireland escapade, my sanity and/or credibility were in question with just about everyone. Farrell had been sweet about the money, probably because I'd returned every penny of it. But asking for a loan now, even a little one, was pushing it to the "Are you kidding?" level. Los was good for a local ride, but even without my injury, I doubted I'd survive the trip to PA with his driving. Even discussing the trip could be dangerous. I didn't know who might rat me out in the name of protecting me.

Oddly enough, it was Dad who solved my problem.

My digital alarm clock displayed the ungodly hour of 6:34 am on Saturday morning when I was awakened by an unusual amount of kitchen activity. I was reluctantly facing a day of watching movies in my room as I painfully climbed out of bed and made my way down the hall.

"You're supposed to be in bed!" Mike scowled as he flipped a pancake.

"I heard noise. You three are up early. What's going on?"

"I've got to go to work today. I've been missing too much with all the craziness and I gotta catch up."

"And I'm going away for the day. Band festival in upstate New York!" Dylan looked as if he'd won the lottery. He really loved band.

"What about you, Brian?"

"Academic decathlon at Stevens Institute today. My brain is so gonna kick ASS!"

Mike poured more batter on the griddle. "Want a pancake?"

"Nah. Hey, D! If you're going away all day, mind if I play Skyrim in your room?"

"Be my guest."

I went to the bathroom, threw some water on my face, and started up to Dylan's room. Walking up the stairs hurt a little. Taking a deep breath hurt a lot.

"Mike! Is that you?" Dad called from his room.

"Nah, Dad. It's me."

"C'mon in a minute."

"I don't want to give you my germs," I sneezed a fake sneeze. Even that gave me a pain in my side but I was doing a smashing job of hiding the accident. My brothers and I had agreed to use a relapse as the excuse to buy me the time that I needed to stay home without letting on to Dad. I did not want to blow it.

"I know, I know. You don't have to come near me. Just open the door a little."

I poked my head in. Dad was in bed looking as pale as powder. I felt a twinge of sadness mixed with anger.

"Take my car keys off the dresser over there, will you?" He motioned towards them. "Tell Mike to use my car today and to drop it off at the gas station across the street from his office.

It needs an oil change."

"Okay," I said brightly, then sniffed loudly for effect. "How are you feeling?" I took the cold metal keys from the dresser and slid them into the pocket of the sweatpants I was wearing.

"Not bad, really. How about you?"

"Still, (sniff!) still got this miserable flu (cough!)." Coughing hurt. I clutched my side but shot my hand down to my stomach, a plan forming swiftly in my desperate little brain. "And....um...and I've got *really* bad cramps too. I think I'm going to (sneeze!) take a couple of aspirin and stay in bed all day today. Do you mind?"

"No. I'm doing okay. A nurse is coming around lunch time. You just rest up." He turned over on his side and his lids fluttered closed a bit. Poor dad, he looked ten years older than he had before I left for Dublin.

"You rest up too, dad." I blew him a kiss. "I'm not blowing too hard so...no germs!" The corners of his mouth curled slightly, as if smiling took a great effort. "Please tell the nurse not to wake me if I'm sleeping."

It sounded like Dad mumbled "Will do" as I crept out of the room and padded down the stairs to the foyer where Michael and Dylan were putting on their coats.

"I thought you were going up to Dylan's room? Can't you stay put?" Mike zipped his parka with finality. "There! I'll just go up and check on dad before we leave."

"No! Don't!" I protested, catching my excited tone and quickly tuning it down to "nonchalant". "I just peeked in his room and he's sound asleep. Let him rest."

"Yeah, and we gotta hurry, Mike! The bus is leaving at 7:00! With me or without me. Mr. DiGioia said! Latecomers get left in the dust!"

"Okay. I'll let him sleep. Did he look...okay?"

"Yep, fine. I went over to the bed. He's...breathing and everything. Fine. Really. I checked on him. Don't worry."

That seemed to satisfy Mike. He ushered Dylan out the door.

"I might not be home until six or so. Dylan's getting a ride home late too." He stopped on the threshold and looked at me with a serious expression. "You okay?"

Just what I needed, Mike to be getting perceptive.

"I'll be fine. I'll just be lying on Dylan's bed playing video games all day. Dad said the nurse is coming this afternoon. She'll check him out and take care of anything he needs."

"She even made him lunch the other day. I think she's sweet on him," threw in Brian charging in behind me. He grabbed his coat off the banister and breezed out the door in one fluid motion calling a hasty "Bye!" over his shoulder.

"See? Don't worry. We'll be fine."

I let out a sigh of relief when the door closed behind them. Then I scurried down the hall to my room to pick out an outfit that would be suitable for when I got arrested for grand theft auto.

*

Once on the road I thought my hasty plan was pretty lame. I had stuffed my bed with pillows like some stupid teen movie stunt and taped a hasty note to my door to discourage Dad's nurse, just in case.

"Took two Midol. Really feel crampy. Please let me sleep. B."

Lame.

But it was the best I could come up with on short notice. I knew I had about six weeks before I could get a clean bill of health from the doctor and, even if I could get transportation to Philly then, Dad's pale face had told me it was too long a time to wait. As soon as I'd wrapped my fingers around his car keys I considered how Maggie must have felt when she couldn't let go of an idea that was bad for her.

So, there I was on the New Jersey Turnpike - a road upon which most vehicles behave as if they had just jumped off the tracks of Magic Mountain in Disneyworld - with a learner's permit and seven hours of actual driving experience. None within the past month. I had pains in my side, the address on the passenger seat, and about twenty three dollars in my pack. My stomach was rolling and my hands were sticking to the steering wheel. And I hadn't even gotten to the first toll booth.

It took me almost three hours to reach the outskirts of Philly where The Tea Fairy made a pretty addition to a little strip mall on a tree lined street. I pulled in the lot and parked where I had a good view of the pink-curtained window front.

Whew! I felt relieved to turn off the ignition. The dashboard clock said 10:34. The sign in the door said "Closed". I bit my lip, wondering what new crime I would commit if I found out I'd come all that way for nothing.

I sat there for a few minutes, taking deep breaths to calm myself down, then opened the car door, and went up to the store front to read the smaller sign with the store hours. It opened for luncheon and tea service at eleven.

Maggie's shop was a frilly place. The ruffled curtains tied back on each side of the window were made of a tiny floral print fabric. Everything was displayed on crocheted doilies or little lacey tea cloths. And everything was ready for Christmas. Boxes of specialty teas and little floral tea pots were tied with red and green ribbons to remind the viewer of what a good gift they might make for a tea lover. Odd little spoons and other contraptions that looked like strainers were placed here and there next to neatly calligraphed signs that said "Stocking stuffers!". Crystal snowflakes were strewn amongst mugs and tea sets of all descriptions. And there were baskets brimming with neat paper bags filled with teas I'd never heard of. What the heck was rooibos?

A cold wind whipped up, whistling shrilly through the trees. I pulled my jacket closer and ran back to the car as fast as my aching side would tolerate. I couldn't wait for the store to open to get a hot cup of coffee! Did they serve coffee?

I felt like a detective on a stake-out, watching the door anxiously for signs of my great aunt. In a few minutes a car pulled up and a petite, Asian girl emerged. She walked to the front door and opened it.

I walked back to the front door. Best to try to talk to someone before any customers arrived. But, when I peeped in, the Asian girl was nowhere to be seen. The wind was relentless and I was about to return to the relative warmth of my dad's car when she appeared from the back with a tray of cakes. I tapped hard on the glass door panel. She looked up and shook a finger at me, shouting "Eleven o'clock" loud enough for me to hear through a brick wall, much less glass. She didn't look happy.

She rushed back and forth from the back room, brought cookies and pastries, filled pots with water, set paper placemats on the tiny tables.

"Excuse me, do you have the time?"

I turned to see a petite, grey-haired woman behind me. She was dressed in a neat pea coat and slacks. I checked my cell phone. "10:43," I muttered. My teeth were chattering and my side ached. The woman glanced in the window at the Asian girl who was now setting tea cups down hastily on the tables.

"Oh, it's Amy. She always gets here late."

"Maybe I'd better go back to the car and wait if she's going to open up late." I started to stamp my feet but every stamp sent a little bolt of pain to my side.

"She'd better not open up late. Rachel will fire her."

"Rachel?"

"The owner. She's also the baker. Is this your first time here?"

191

"Um, yes."

"Lovely cakes and pastries. Worth the wait, really."

"Do you know the owner?"

"Not personally but my grand-daughter, Nicole, worked here over the summer. She said Rachel is a stickler about punctuality."

The woman tapped her foot impatiently, staring at Amy who was moving like a tornado. "Ooh! She almost dropped a cup. That girl is going to lose her job if she doesn't shape up. Rachel doesn't like her employees to rush. She likes them to get here early and get everything done neatly and professionally, the European way."

My ears pricked. "Is Rachel from Europe?"

"Yes. From France. She makes the most wonderful La Religieuse. Have you ever heard of that? It means "The Nun" because it's shaped like a French nun's hat. Of course, not a modern one. Filled with the most divine chocolate."

My mouth started to water. And my mind started to race. Great Aunt Molly had told me about her sister's Parisian store.

"I'm going to sit in the car. It is nippy today, isn't it?" chirped the woman, gripping her collar. "And the wind is howling so oddly."

*

A few minutes later I was beating the old lady to the door. Amy was setting a marker down next to a small whiteboard at the entrance. Promptly at ten, she turned like an automaton and opened the door with the most annoyed look on her face. Then, as if she were auditioning for the part of "gracious hostess", she wiped the scowl off and smiled broadly.

"Welcome to The Tea Fairy!"

"Is Rachel here?" I blurted. Amy looked surprised.

"She just left for the day. She always leaves right after the shop is set up for opening. We're not hiring if that's..."

"Can you call her?"

Amy looked as if I'd suggested that we blow up the Pentagon.

"I don't have her number," she stumbled. She was fibbing.

"What about emergencies, don't you..."

"Ah, Amy. Good morning! When you're finished seating this young lady, I'll have my usual. With rooibos tea today." It was pea coat lady, bright as a ray of sunshine. Amy smiled again.

"Of course, Mrs. Castanzo!" she grinned. Then, turning back to me, she offered a slightly less pleasant, "Would you like to sit down or not?"

"I'll have a La Religieuse. Chocolate. And coffee..."

"We don't have coffee, we..."

"Rooibos. I'll try that one."

*

There's just so much time you can kill eating a pastry. I figured I'd wait until the woman was done with her usual (oddly enough, the same as my usual) and then I'd corner Amy alone. Unfortunately for me, The Tea Fairy, was a very busy place and it was full of customers before I slipped the last delicious morsel of chocolate and pâte à chou into my mouth. At $6.95 I wasn't going to have another one.

Across the street from the strip mall was a book store. It seemed a good, warm, place to hide until business at the tea shop dwindled. But, after several trips back and forth to check out the clientele, it looked like closing time might be my only chance. That meant staying until 5:30 p.m., which meant getting home by eight or later. Which was not going to work.

It was just after the lunch hour rush when I returned to the tea shop. A slight, blonde-haired waitress was serving tea to two shoppers in the corner. Amy was at the register.

"Can I help you?"

"Yes. I really need to speak with Rachel."

"I told you, I don't have her number."

"What if there's an emergency? You don't have a way to call the owner during an emergency?"

Amy rolled her eyes. She looked extremely annoyed.

I spied a pile of matchboxes in a bowl next to the register. They all sported pictures of a fairy drinking a cup of tea. "What if...," I opened a box, lit a match, and held it up to a paper menu display at the counter. "What if there's a fire here? Or....," I glanced around a little wildly, "what if some crazy person starts smashing every tea cup on the shelf!?"

"Then I call the police," smirked Amy, unperturbed by my bluff.

"Fair enough," I replied, shaking out the

match. I decided upon a new tack. "Listen. Maybe you do have my...Rachel's number, and maybe you don't. But, if you do, why don't you call her up and tell her that there's a girl here who was sent by Mrs. O'Hora of Dun Laoghaire. See what she says."

Amy looked skeptical.

"I'm serious, Amy. She might be upset with you if she finds out I was here and you *didn't* call her!"

She looked down at her watch and then glanced back up at me quizzically. "Dun....what?"

"Here. I'll write it down." I pulled a pen from my pack and grabbed a paper menu. "I'll write it like you say it...done - leery. Mrs. O'Hora. I'll just walk back across the street to the book store for, say, half an hour? That should give you plenty of time to find Rachel's number, no? If I come back and she doesn't want to see me, I'll go home. How's that?"

Amy wrinkled her mouth into a wry expression but she took the paper. "We'll see."

*

The half hour passed quickly. I had just lifted myself from the comfort of an overstuffed armchair and was walking towards the exit when I felt a sharp tap on my shoulder.

"Excuse me. Are you looking for Rachel Fournier?"

The accent was French, but it was a put on; I knew instantly that I was looking at my great-aunt. If the cascade of red hair held back on one side by a golden comb did not make the

195

introduction, the small, heart-shaped mole on the woman's lip told me that I was facing Maggie Connor in the flesh. There was no mistaking her resemblance to the photo I'd seen at my aunt's in Dun Laoghaire. My jaw dropped in surprise and a goose-bumpy little chill of shock ran through me.

"Maggie?"

The woman turned white as her baking flour. "Let's go outside. I don't want to talk een here." It was a command, not an invitation, because she immediately did an about face and walked out the door. I followed her out where the wind was churning up debris in the street and the sky had gone steel grey, glad for the remnants of warmth inside her van, a large, pink delivery truck with the Tea Fairy logo emblazoned on the side.

"How do you know Meesus. O'Hora?" She looked angry in spite of her forced smile.

"She's my great-aunt. I met her in Dublin. You're..." My voice trailed off. I had rehearsed what I was going to say to her hundreds of times but this meeting was a little bit different than I had expected. "I'm Bridget Anne Connor. My father is Peter and Katherine Connor's oldest son. Molly O'Hora is my great aunt."

A strong gust rocked the van slightly. Maggie started the engine and turned on the heat. "I'd razher not stay here. Let's go to my house for a cup of tea, shall we? We can talk in privacy and comfort."

I pulled my cell phone from my pocket. It was already two forty-five. I figured I could push it until five o'clock the latest before I would have to leave.

"Who are you calling?" she said nervously.

"I was just checking the time. I have to get the car home before my brothers get hone at seven. They don't know I took the car ..." I bit my stupid tongue.

"Don't worry. Eet's not far and I'm sure we can straighten all this out queekly."

Maggie's demeanor was understandable. I'd busted into her cozy little world; she wasn't going to let her guard down instantaneously. Her phony French accent, however, was getting on my nerves.

I decided to drop conversation until we were in a more relaxed atmosphere.

In about twenty minutes the van pulled off the street down a long, tree-lined drive that led behind a well-cared-for, Victorian home. I grabbed the light pack I was carrying and followed her into the back entrance. From the second she entered the kitchen, it was clear that she was in her element. Her face was composed and relaxed as she began bustling about, throwing her keys on the counter, pulling off her jacket, putting on tea water.

"Seet down, please! What kind do you like?" She offered a basket of teas of every flavor. I rummaged through the labels and found some chai. At least I knew what that was. Soon she presented me with a floral china cup that wafted the scent of exotic spices. I sipped it slowly as she prepared a tray of cookies.

Maggie's kitchen was cute and cozy and her home was nearly as frilly as her tea shop. My idea of appealing to this woman's better nature to escape the hardship of her fate suddenly seemed utterly ludicrous to me. Who was going to willingly give up a successful business, a lovely home, and eternal youth?

"Zere now," she said, settling across the table from me and placing the plate down, "why don't you tell me your story. What did Meesus O'Hora tell you, exactly?"

I grabbed a cookie topped with raspberry jam to offset the slightly bitter taste of the tea.

"Listen, you can drop the phony accent. And don't be mad at Molly for telling me where you are. I'd traveled a long way to see her." For the first time, I was able to examine my great-aunt's face in detail. Her hair was the color of the sun setting in July and her eyes were sapphire blue. But the most remarkable thing about her face was that she looked no older than any college girl I knew. "Aunt Molly didn't have to tell me much. I already knew about the comb. I know what happened with the banshee. I went to Dublin to find you..."

She laughed as if I were telling a joke. "Me? To find me?" She waved a hand dismissively. "I've never been to Dublin een my life and I don't know what ees these banchee!"

I glanced at my cell phone. It was almost 3: 30. "Please, don't make this difficult. I haven't got a lot of time. I *know* who you are."

"Of course you do! I'm Rachel Fournier, zee owner of Zeh Tea Fairy!"

I felt the angry blood pounding in my temples. "You're Molly O'Hora's sister, Maggie. You're my great aunt. You left Ireland..."

"Meesus O'Hora ees an old friend of zeh

family. She was very close to my mozher." visited my maman een France years ago when I was born. She stood up as my godmozher when I was baptized. We've been in touch ever since. She's a sweet old woman but I don't think she's - how do you say it? - playing wiz a fool deck, eef you know what I mean. She always says I resemble some long lost relative of hers, eesn't zat somesing? But I have no idea what you're talking about."

"God's kiss, Aunt Maggie! God's kiss!"

Maggie's face blanched again.

"The comb in your hair! I saw your picture with Molly and Fionan. I know who you are!" I shouted, rising to my feet and slamming both hands on the table so hard that a jolt of pain whipped me in the side. "I've got two brothers and a father whose lives are in danger because of that goddamn comb you're wearing! Your nephew Aidan *died* about a month and a half ago because of you! You're Maggie Connor, from Sligo, you're seventy-seven years old, and it's time for you to put an end to this!"

My great aunt just stared at me, white and quiet. Suddenly, a wave of nausea gripped me and I felt foggy-headed and tired. I slumped back into the kitchen chair. This wasn't from my injury.

"What did you do?"

"It's just a little somesing to make you relax. You are too excited."

I felt myself falling, falling. The room was spinning. The last thing I heard was Maggie's voice, sans accent, saying: "And I needed some time to think.

Chapter 11 - Buried Alive

I couldn't figure out where I was at first. All I knew was it felt like Metallica had done a year-long farewell tour inside my head and my ribs stung like hell. It was dark and cool and my wrist was tightly chained to...a boiler pipe? A hot water heater? Why didn't I pay more attention to those contraptions at home? Not that it mattered much. What I should have paid closer attention to was every James Bond film that had ever come out because it was going to take something like his mastermind to figure a way out of this one. The chain was attached to my wrist with a lock. Could I pick the lock? Pull on the chain? Would the damn pipe I was attached to explode in my face with boiling steam if I broke it?

I was lying on some towels on the floor of a basement. Didn't need MI6 to figure that one out. I sat up to get a better look at my surroundings but my head and side hurt so much I fell back down again. The headache had to be from whatever drug Great Aunt Maggie had slipped into my tea but I could think of no explanation for the hideous pain in my ribs that didn't make me contemplate the necessity of drawing up a will. The doctor had given me all the usual scary medical warnings about breaking my rib through, piercing a lung, internal injuries. I tried to take a deep breath. I couldn't.

A Glade candle burned next to a tray of cookies on top of a washing machine. In spite of the pain, I slid the chain up the pipe and struggled to my knees. I had no interest in food but there was a piece of paper propped up on the tray, just within reach.

I work nights. I will be down with breakfast when I come in.

Breakfast? Sunday breakfast? How long had I been out? I groped around the floor in the dim light and found my pack. Of course, my phone was gone. Maggie was smart; she'd even removed the metal buttons and my pen; so much for James Bond tools. And there isn't a high school girl in the United States who still uses hair pins, so picking the lock was out of the question unless it could be accomplished with gum wrappers and tampons.

Crap! My brothers had to be freaking out. The police were probably out searching for me and Dad's car. For one delusional moment I was glad I had parked it in a busy strip mall out in full view of the street.

The keys. Where were the keys? My aunt had taken those too. The car was probably at the bottom of the Wissahickon by now.

Pain bit me in the side so fiercely that I crumpled onto the cold, cement floor and pulled some towels over me. Nausea and dizziness took over. It might have been the boiler running or some piece of basement machinery, but before I blacked out again in the gloom and the cold, I thought I heard the banshee wail.

*

A dim, grayish light filtering in from the ground level window behind me told me it was dawn. My head still ached but I managed to prop myself up just enough to survey my surroundings a little better.

The chain on my wrist was looped and attached twice to one of the pipes in the back of the room by the boiler and hot water heater. A narrow door stood ajar in the center of the left wall. I could just see part of the toilet inside. A bathroom. Great. A lot of good it did me with two feet of slack.

The washer and dryer sat along the right wall, and a closed and, I could only guess, locked door was about three feet away from my heels. A laundry room. I tried to turn around behind me to see if I could get a clear look through the narrow basement window. If a house was close enough they might hear me.

I inhaled to scream but the pain caught my breath and all I could manage was a weak, fading wail that disappeared from my throat, only to be picked up by another wail.

"Eeeeeeeeeeeeeeeeeeoooaaaaaaaaaa!"

The ectoplasmic intruder floated right through the door. Old Red Eyes. Every single hair follicle in my body went into goosebump mode. A chill colder than the cement floor covered me as she slid towards me like a film over water. It seemed to take her ages to move from the door, as her form collected itself, finally arriving at its terrifying destination over my body. She floated down like fog, covering me in cold and fear. I could see her bones through the milky veil.

"She muuuust give it!" her voice like a sandy wind blown across a desert. "She muuuuuuuuuust or I will take yooooooooouuuuuuurss."

She took a bony finger and stuck it in my side. It was like being stabbed with an icicle and I screamed in agony, a shriek that joined with the banshee's cry, and faded in pain even as she did into a wisp. The room was clammy in her wake and a scent like dead roses filled the air.

I lay cringing in the pile of towels, terrified. I knew what her words meant.

*

A few moments later, a door slammed. There were footfalls on the stairs and Great Aunt Maggie walked in as calmly as if she were going to church.

"It won't do yeh any good to scream," she said with just the faintest touch of brogue, "no one is going to hear you. Or did you forget how long my driveway is?"

"It wasn't me. It was the banshee."

"Bullshit!" she blurted, her wide eyes betraying her fear.

"She was just here. You heard the banshee."

"I heard yeh screamin' like one," she composed herself, pulled a low wooden stool from the corner near the door and sat at my feet, "so I came down to save yeh the trouble of a sore throat. Screaming is useless, Bridget. And unnecessary, really. I don't mean you any harm."

"Drugging me is your idea of no harm?"

"I'm sorry, I really am. I didn't know what to do. I wasn't sure of who you were or why you were here."

"I wanted to try to get you to end the curse."

"So my sister Molly told me."

"You talked with her?"

"I called her last night. Crazy old bat verified that you were looking for me because of that sorry tale about a family curse and banshees. Ridiculous."

"Then why trap me down here then? Where's your French accent? Why did you fake it if you're not running from something?"

Maggie sighed deeply and stared at the ground for a long moment.

"Well, as for the accent. It's good fer business. Who ever heard of famous Irish pastries? And as for kidnappin' yeh, I'm truly sorry. I've been hidin' from a maniac ex-husband and I didn't know if he'd sent yeh. That's all. I don't want my cover blown. I've been runnin' from him for years. It has nothin' to do with all this nonsense about curses and banshees. Yer as nuts as old Molly if yeh think so."

"So why don't you just hand over that gold comb you're wearing for a few minutes if there's nothing to the curse."

"Well, dear, perhaps because this comb has been a great blessing to me rather than a curse."

"So," I jangled the chain on the pipe, "I'm not exactly going to run away with it."

"It's...it's a little superstition of mine. I wear it always. It belonged to my

204

grandmother...."

"Grandmother Mary? The one you let die for it?"

"She did not die because of this...!"

"Gotcha, Aunt Maggie."

Maggie crossed her arms and went silent for a long time. I didn't trust it. It reminded me of Molly at the sink, buying time and concocting a story in her head.

"Alright. So what if I am yer Great Aunt," she said finally. "And what if this business about the comb is true? What do yeh intend to do about it? Do yeh want the comb for yerself?"

The slightest giggle escaped my lips but my side seared even with that small movement; I grabbed it with my one free hand and let out a little cry of pain.

"What's wrong?"

"I had a few cracked ribs when I came here. I wasn't even supposed to be out of the house. Tell me. How'd you get me onto this floor? In spite of a magic comb, I don't expect you floated me down the steps."

"I'm sorry. I didn't know! I didn't mean to hurt yeh."

"Well, maybe you did and maybe you didn't. But I don't want your comb for myself. I want it because I'm worried about my two brothers in the hospital, my dad who just had a heart attack. I'm worried they'll wind up like Aidan because of you and that comb..."

My aunt got up so violently that she knocked over the stool.

"That's ridiculous? Why does everythin' that happens to a Connor come to be my blame?

I don't even know yer family. And I never even met my nephew Aidan. Until today I hadn't had any news of the family in Ireland in ages so I hardly knew he was alive much less dead."

"I saw him die, you know."

"How could yeh...?"

"He died in New York, Maggie. At a club where I was singing. I didn't know who he was, but it was here, in this country. In October. Shortly after you came to the states. Coincidence, no? That's just when my family's troubles started too..."

"Yer lyin'!"

"Didn't Molly tell you any of this?"

"I just asked her who yeh were and why yeh were at my door and she started babbling about seeing a banshee and the curse and said you thought you could get me to stop it." Maggie shook her head and laughed. "I hung up on her." Then she rose from the stool. "But even if the curse was real, I doubt you could come up with some idea that hasn't crossed my mind these many years. True or not, there's nothing to be done about it because the banshee doesn't want the comb back. She told me so. And why should I give it to yeh? Do you think I'm stupid? I bet yeh'd like to look like a rock star for the next forty years. That would give yeh a lot of time to work on your singin' career, wouldn't it?"

With that, she walked out the door and locked it behind her.

*

The idea of rotting in a basement did not

206

appeal to me but struggling against the chains was of no use because all that did was send all kinds of electric pain through my chest area. This felt worse than something caused by falling five feet off of the high school stage, it was more like I fell off a building. I was furious with frustration, contenting myself only with the progress of having gotten Maggie to admit to who she was. Whether that would shorten my stay or lengthen it, I had no idea.

It wasn't very long before the grey dawn displayed promise of a bright winter day. The door opened and my great aunt stepped in with a pretty tea tray heaped with quiche, fruit, and pastries.

"Here yeh are. I'm not the monster yeh may think me to be."

I felt sick to my stomach and waved off the tray. "I don't feel well. I'm in a lot of pain. Really. I'm not just saying that to play you. Take a look at my ribs."

I lifted my free hand behind my head and tugged my shirt up. She put the tray on the dryer and leaned over me cautiously.

"Where does it...oh!"

"What, oh? What's wrong?" Contrary to Lisa DeLotto's opinion, my boobs were not so flat that I could see under them very well.

"Was it... always like this?"

"Like what? I had some bruises that showed but, I don't know if it's worse. I can't see."

Maggie went to the bathroom and returned with a small cosmetic mirror.

"Can yeh see it?" she said, holding it to my

ribs. I adjusted the angle slightly. The skin looked as if a pot of bloody purple dye had erupted beneath the surface.

"That looks a *lot* worse than it did a couple of days ago. I think I need to get home." I nodded towards the open door and tugged at my chain slightly. "But right now I need to use the bathroom. Really badly. Any chance of that?"

"I can loosen the chain and let you walk around a bit. But don't go trying to yank at it and run off."

I rolled my eyes. "Do I look like I'm in any shape to run?"

"So you promise?"

"I just want to wash my face and pee! I promise I won't try to leave!"

She hesitated an instant before she walked over and put the key in the first lock at the pipe. The loop of chain dropped open, giving me about enough room to reach the bathroom and maybe four feet out the door that Maggie was now blocking.

If she had any doubt about my intentions, they had to have been erased as she watched my slow and painful amble to the bathroom where I washed my face and hands, soaked a small guest towel with cold water, wrung it out, and pressed it to my side. Trying to walk back was even more difficult as I fought dizziness, nausea.

My great aunt was by the dryer, folding the towels I'd lain on. She took a long look at me standing slumped up against the door jamb, holding my side.

"I'll be right back," she said, bustling out again and returning not five minutes later with a bottle of aspirin, a second tea cup, and two folding chairs. She set the chairs near the washer and dryer and gave me her arm to help me sit in one.

"What time is it?"

"It's Sunday morning, around 9:30."

"My family is going to be looking everywhere for me."

"Well......" there was that pause again, "maybe not." She took the tea pot off the tray on the dryer and started pouring. "Michael texted your phone last night, asking 'Where are you, sis?'. I relayed the message that you were sorry about the car and had gone to New York City to see a concert and were staying with some friends."

With my current erratic behavior, Michael just might believe that.

"What are you planning on telling him about today? 'Hi Mike! I'm in the hotel room partying with the band. Don't wait dinner for me.'?" That'll go over big."

"I don't think that will be necessary. I also told him your battery was down to 6% so you were shutting your phone, and you'd be home tonight. And I think you can be if we can straighten all this out." She handed me the tea cup in one hand and put two pills in the other. "This should help a little."

I looked at the items suspiciously.

"It's just tea and aspirin." Maggie popped one of the pills and took a sip from the cup. "Although I don't blame yeh for doubting me."

I chased the capsule down with a warm sip of tea.

"Look, Maggie, I want to go home. If you let me go I won't tell anyone what happened or where you are, I promise. But, if you'd please hear me out, I do have an idea of how to end the curse." Long shot though it seemed after getting a good look at my great aunt's life, I'd come too far not to try.

Her face went sour. "I told yeh this mornin'. Yeh can't have the comb."

"I don't want the frikkin' comb! That's not what I came here for!" I said as emphatically as the pain permitted. "I want you to stop the curse!"

Maggie sighed like someone frustrated with a small child throwing a tantrum.

"Go ahead. I'll give yeh two minutes. After that *you* listen, fair enough?"

I nodded. "Okay. When Aidan died my dad told me the story of the comb and the curse. I didn't really believe it until it hit home and two of my brothers had horrible accidents. Then my dad had a heart attack." Against my will, the tears just started to pour out. In spite of everything, I was furious with myself.

"I went to Dublin to find you. To tell you..." A wave of nausea hit me hard and my breath came in short, fast gasps. I was sure I was having a panic attack, gripped with the realization that the words I wanted to say were – had been all along – nothing more than the desperate straw-grasping of a high school girl who couldn't accept the fact that her family was doomed. Convince Great Aunt Maggie to leave a life where her only troubles were running from her ex and looking too young and pretty? I gulped down the sick feeling and let the words spill out anyway.

"The thing is, this banshee only wants out. She just wants to stop mourning for the Connors because...because you pissed her off. Because she wants release, to go into the light, whatever the reason. Who knows? The important thing is, the curse says she isn't going to be happy until the last Connor of our line dies out and her job is done. Well, with my dad, five brothers, and my five uncles and their boys, that's a lot of dying ahead. Do you think it's fair to have all that life wasted so you can stay eternally young?"

Maggie sighed very heavily. "Bridget, that question isn't one I haven't asked myself sometimes when I think of what happened all those years ago, the way this comb changed my life, the accusations the family have made against me." She started to rub her hands together nervously. "I wasn't there when my brother's children passed. I didn't know them and I didn't see them die. I'm still not certain that their deaths weren't coincidence or bad luck but, even if all this curse nonsense was true, I already told yeh, she wouldn't take the comb back. I wasn't lyin' about that. I really tried. She doesn't want it!"

"Yes, but what if you have something else she wants?"

My great aunt looked confused. "And what could that be?"

I took a deep breath, shaking from cold, from fear, from pain and from the prospect of finally getting to say the words I'd been carrying with me for her, and hearing them spill out to a reception of laughter and dismissal.

"What if you took her place?"

"Took her place? Am I to be after killing myself now? "

"I don't think so. But I know that's what she wants."

Maggie's eyes narrowed and she made a wry face. "And how do yeh know that?"

"The banshee told me."

*

Not so surprisingly, Maggie did not want to explore my idea. She wouldn't even listen to me once I stated it but left the laundry again, tray in hand and I didn't see her until later that day when she came down with lunch and found me lying on the floor again in sickness and defeat.

"I'm in no shape to eat. I think I've got a fever. I may be dying."

Maggie laughed. "From rock star to actress. Yeh are a talented young lady, aren't yeh?"

I struggled up onto my elbows, coughing. "I'm not kidding. The banshee said it was my life or yours. And you've made the choice." I struggled up onto my elbows, coughing.

"Banshee my ass! Look! I gave yeh a chance to state yer case this mornin', didn't I?"

"I suppose so. Most of it."

"And yeh said yeh'd listen to me?"

I nodded.

"Alright, then. Here's my story. I have spent a lifetime runnin' away from the blame of the so-called Connor Curse. I'll admit there is somethin' magical about the comb, I mean, just

212

look at me. But as far as the deaths go? I'm not so sure that was my doin' at all. If the banshee gave me no choice but to keep the comb, how can I be blamed for not stopping it?

"I didn't know my brother's babies and I didn't know Aidan, but I knew he was reachin' his twenty-first birthday. So, when the chance came to move to the states I took it and thought, if the curse was indeed real, my leavin' Ireland might end it. And Aidan comes here. Well then, it seems there's no escapin' it."

"But what if you can stop it from happening again? The banshee didn't want her comb back but maybe you can throw it away, deny its power...."

"Listen! This is my side of the story! Yeh had yer turn. And I'm tellin' yeh that even if yer idea did work, why should I give up everythin' I have? Why should I give up eternal life for a bunch of distant relations I've never met? Give me one good reason. Why?"

Wracked with pain, it felt like the floor was coming up through my ribs and I could barely breathe my answer before I passed out.

"To save your own soul."

*

When I woke up it was dusky again. Sunday evening, I figured. Or maybe a rainy Sunday afternoon. Either way, no doubt about the trouble I was causing back home now.

My great aunt's shop was closed on Mondays so she wouldn't be running off to bake. That meant that I might have the chance to speak with her at supper. Or in the morning?

There was a soft, fluffy blanket over me now - I curled my fingers around it in the dark - and a pillow under my head. The ground felt just a bit softer. Or was I getting used to it? In the distance I heard bagpipes, harps. Was I in Irish heaven or was Maggie playing some Celtic music?

Maggie's familiar footsteps approached and she came in with another tray. Some kind of soup, chips, more tea and cookies.

"Here, try to eat this. I don't want anythin' to happen to yeh."

"Something will happen to me, Aunt Maggie." My own voice sounded hollow and distant. "I'm going to die. The banshee said it was you or me. If you won't take her place, I'll have to. And I will. To save my brothers, my dad, I will."

"Oh stop the drama. You're going to be fine. Here!" She set the tray down and stuck a spoon of soup near my mouth. I hadn't eaten all day so I took a sip. Then another. But I couldn't get much down before the nausea hit again and I had to wave it off.

"I want to go home." Even as I said the words I couldn't imagine how I could do it.

Maggie set the tray aside. "Listen," she crossed her arms in front of herself resolutely, "I've given things some thought. If you send anyone after me I'm going to deny keepin' you here against your will, y'know. It's my word against yours. I'll tell them that you came here ranting about Ireland and banshees. That isn't likely to go well for you, Bridget."

"Fair enough. They've been doubting my

sanity since I ran off to Ireland so you wouldn't have much trouble convincing them I'd lost it. And I don't want to put my family through any more trouble. I'll tell them I just had to get away, that I snapped from the pressure of everything that is going on at home, that I didn't come home because I got sick. You have my dad's car?"

"I do. It's out back."

I looked out the basement window. Winter darkness was already falling. It wasn't going to be fun driving home but I pushed off the covers and tried to sit up. And threw up all over the basement floor. Maggie frowned.

"Maybe I should leave in the morning. The roads are dark and unfamiliar, and I don't think I'm well enough to drive right now." It was an understatement.

My great aunt cocked one eyebrow. "Or old enough from the learner's permit I found in yer wallet. But I don't know if it's a good thing for you to stay. It's getting late and your family is bound to start asking questions. Your text said that you were coming home tonight. If you don't want to worry them, you should go."

She seemed nervous. As much as she had threatened about making me look bad, she had to know that the discovery of my dead body in her home wasn't going to look good for her. She was as anxious to get rid of me as I was to go but I felt too sick to move much less brave the New Jersey Turnpike in the dark. I knew I was failing. Maybe I could make it a few blocks to a gas station, to a phone. But I wasn't sure I could make it out the door. I needed someone to come for me.

Suddenly, an idea hit me.

"Is my phone still working?"

"I turned it off after I sent the last text. It should be."

"Text Mike. Say, 'Staying at Abigail's for a few days.' That will cover it, and when I show up tomorrow, so much the better. Abigail's a good friend. She's covered for me before. If they call her she'll think I'm spending the night with my boyfriend, Farrell, and she'll swear I'm walking her dog or in her shower. She's good for that sort of thing. My dad," I winked, "typical Irish father. Thinks his daughter is still a virgin."

Maggie hesitated only slightly, pulled my phone from her pocket, turned it on, and looked for Mike's number in the contact list. "Okay. 'Stayin' at Abigail's for a couple of days.' Is that it?"

"That should do it," I said. *I hope that does it*, I thought.

Chapter 12 - White Wails

It was dark when I dragged myself up off the floor. I could barely stand but I had to pee. And I was short-chained again.

CLANK! CLANK! I smacked the loose chain against the pipe.

"MAAAAAAGIEEEEEE! MAAAAAAGIEEEEEEE!" I only had to keep up the ruckus for about three minutes before I heard her storming down the steps.

"Okay! Okay! Yeh'll raise the dead with that racket!"

"I don't have to bang on a pipe to raise the dead. It seems to come naturally."

"What's the noise about?"

"I have to go to the bathroom. I've already thrown up on your floor; I didn't want to add any more bodily fluids."

"Listen, why don't yeh come upstairs and use the bathroom and sleep in a warm bed? You can leave in the morning." Her attitude seemed to be softening. Either that or she figured out that finding my dead body safe and comfy in a warm bed would look a little better to the authorities than finding it on the basement floor chained to a pipe.

"That sounds like a plan," I said, struggling to stand.

She helped me up every painful step up the stairs, through her kitchen, and down her hall to the bathroom. I did my business and waited inside while she fetched an oversized tee shirt for me to slip into. My clothes had some vomit on them so I didn't protest. When I came out, she was standing outside the door.

"Want some tea now?"

"I drank a little water in the bathroom, I'm good."

She got me settled into a room with a four-poster bed covered in a pink and blue chintz bedspread. A small light was on at the bed stand. There was a clock, some photos.

"I'll wash and dry your clothes early tomorrow so you can go home fresh," she said as she smoothed the covers over.

My head was already down on the pillow, my thanks muffled.

"I'm sorry about all this, Bridget. I really didn't mean to hurt you."

I opened my eyes and met Maggie's. "I think I understand. You've been hiding a long time. I was a threat. It's okay. I'll go home and it will be like this never happened." I let my gaze wander around the room. Ruffled curtains with bows. Flower vases. Lots of pink. "Aunt Molly would love this room," I mused.

"How is she? I didn't ask her last night. All I did was scream at her." She looked regretful.

Maggie was lonely. That much was clear. Her loneliness both a protection and part of her curse. How close can you get to people when you have to keep leaving them? It occurred to me that my great aunt had gotten only a shadow of the love she craved.

"She's fine. Takes her daily walks on the pier with Mr. O'Hora in Dun Laoghaire. I'm afraid I gave her a hard time."

"Maybe yeh did. She said you were very

persistent. I don't think she said that to excuse what she did, giving me away and all. I could tell she admired yer spunk. She liked you."

"I liked her too." Groggy thoughts of Dublin drifted through my head. "She saw the banshee too, you know."

"She mentioned that you two had...an incident in Christchurch Cathedral. She said she saw a white woman with her hand on yer shoulder and that she didn't believe yeh until then." Maggie sat down and sighed. "Truth be told, I've spent most of my life tryin' to forget that spectre. Tellin' myself it didn't happen. Tryin' to convince myself that it was imagination. But, every time I look in the mirror, every time people ask questions and I have to leave...."

"It must be difficult to move so often," I began.

"Yes, it is," she sighed, "very difficult." Her eyes wandered over to the nightstand where several gold-framed photos of an adorable little girl with curly red hair and blue eyes were displayed.

"Who's that little girl?"

Maggie lifted a photo of the child dressed in a blue frock and holding a stuffed bear close to her heart. "My daughter, Meghan. I named her after my mother."

"Where is she now?"

"She lives with her father, in Dublin. He's the one looks for me. She's thirty four years old." She placed the photo back down on the credenza. "She thinks I'm dead." She wiped away a stray tear and her voice went deep.

Of course. It made sense. How do you

visit your daughter when you look like you could be *her* daughter?

"Let's get off to bed now, shall we? I'm really tired." She shut the light on the nightstand. The clock there read 1:35. "You know where the bathroom is. I trust this room will be much more comfortable than the laundry room."

Her voice sounded apologetic so I thanked her and watched her walk out the door. As I drifted off, I thought I heard sobbing but I did not have the strength to get up to determine if the sounds were from Maggie's room or another visitation. I was asleep in an instant.

*

Sobbing. Was that what had awakened me in the dark? This time, there was no doubt in my mind that the sounds were otherworldly. In one slow, agonizing motion, I turned over to put on the light, but before I could plant my feet on the ground, the door burst open and Great Aunt Maggie ran to my bedside.

"Make her stop! Can you make her stop?" she cried, tugging my hand.

"Who?"

"The banshee. She's in my room, cryin' and wailin'. She won't stop."

"What makes you think I can stop her?"

"She's callin' you!"

I felt myself going cold from pain and fear and it was only with difficulty that I managed to leave the bed, stumble to the doorway, and lean on the jamb. Through the open door across the hall, I could see my aunt's bed. Sitting at the foot was The Lady. As always, she was combing her hair, silver tears streaming down her cheeks.

"That's mom's banshee."

"Mom's?"

"When my mother died, I saw her. I call her The Lady. She won't hurt you," I said, moving back towards my room.

Maggie grabbed my arm, sending a sharp jolt through my side.

"What do you mean?"

"She's here for me," I said, collapsing in a heap in the hall.

"Bridget! Bridget, are you okay?"

"I don't think so," I said, moving my hand to my right side. It felt swollen and so sore I couldn't even lay a finger on it. "I think I might be bleeding internally."

"I'll call an ambulance for you…" her voice trailed off and her face froze as a high-pitched scream sounded behind me. Maggie's eyes were fixed in a terrified stare just above my head.

"It's her…," she gasped.

"Your banshee?" My breath was labored, words were hard to form.

"Yes," Maggie whispered.

"She's here for me too."

The same terror I'd felt in the basement the previous morning gripped me now as the first pale wisp floated from behind and wind whipped up around me. My vision grew foggy, buzzing sounded in my ears. I felt like I was being swallowed into some icy smoke machine.

As the banshee moved closer, Maggie crawled away from my side to huddle against the wall nearer her bedroom door. "What do you want? Leave her alone!" she screamed.

At the sound of her voice, the wraith flew across the hall towards the cringing Maggie with a windy roar. She threw her hands over her eyes.

"What do you want? I told you I'd return your comb!"

The red-eyed banshee let out a howling wail of laughter and twisted her spidery white fingers into my aunt's hair, trailing its bright tendrils up and up with digits so pale it was as if my aunt's hair was floating of its own accord. The comb began to glow like fire.

"Stop it! Stop it! It burns!" she screamed, tearing at the comb.

With the maleficent, red-eyed creature now occupied with torturing my great-aunt, The Lady flew to my side, throwing herself between me and the horror. The gentle spirit hovered near me, her head turned towards Red Eyes.

"It's alright," I said. "I can't let them all die. I have to go." I reached out to push her away but all I felt was a coolness as my hand slipped through mist. "It's my choice. There's no other way."

I was half mad with pain. It was the sort of pain you cannot believe you will survive, an agony so great that, at that moment, I felt that dying would be a relief.

And at that moment, Red Eyes turned her attention to me once more. She flew towards me with a possessive, violent force so strong that the lovely ghost vanished again.

"Now...now....it's time." Some ectoplasmic ooze drooled from her slash of a mouth as she spoke. "Youuuuuu....youuuuuuuuuu will take my place. Thousands of years and now I will be freeeeeeeee!"

White hands slid over her shoulders as The Lady tore her off. The wind that had been blowing stirred up so strongly that pictures went flying off the walls. One flew down the hall and smashed so fiercely against the bathroom door that glass shards glistened in the wood in the little bit of light that emanated from the open door to my aunt's room.

A small secretary set along the wall next to Maggie's room fell over, spilling its contents, pens and paper flying in tornado formation through the air.

My great aunt moved back to my side and knelt over me as objects whizzed past our faces.

"Can you walk?"

"No, I don't think so. And where would we go? She'll only follow me." With a great deal of effort I lifted my head and turned it towards the direction of the rushing air. The Lady and Red Eyes were inextricably entwined in a mass of swirling white and silver, locked in an epic fight that was tearing apart our reality. The walls bent in and groaned, doors slammed on their hinges, the rug rose and fell off of the floor in waves, what was left of my heart slammed in my throat.

Then...dead quiet. But the silence provided no relief because I could hear my own blood thumping in my ears. In the still air a lone scrap of paper floated down from the ceiling. The rug and walls and doors were once again stationary. A few pictures had righted themselves on the walls.

"What happened?" whispered Maggie, still

huddled over my prone form on the ground. "Is it over?"

"It will neeever be oooover," moaned the banshee, "until I'm freeeeeee!"

Red Eyes appeared above us both, her fingers stretched out to me in long, unnatural tendrils. I felt a paralyzing grip around my throat, and I felt myself spinning down and down a vortex, drowning in darkness. The Lady was waiting for me at the end of the tunnel.

"Bridget! Bridget, stay with me!" My great aunt's voice sounded so, so far away. I gasped for air but none seemed to fill my lungs and the pain brought tears to my eyes. I closed them tightly, feeling hot drops pour down my temples.

"Here! Take me!" Maggie shouted. My eyes fluttered open just enough to see her standing beneath the outstretched arms of Red Eyes whose fingertips were pouring down in ectoplasmic wisps.

Maggie ran her hand through her hair and drew out the comb. It almost paled in the bright locks that were loosed and fell down across her shoulders. "I can't watch her die! I can't have this on my soul for eternity! Here!" And with that Maggie threw the comb at the wraith above her. It bounced against the wall as the apparition vanished.

At first, Great Aunt Maggie just stood there in the quiet hall. Save for the broken picture frame and the comb on the floor, everything seemed to be back to normal. I was almost glad of that one broken frame later, of the glass shards stuck in the wood that made me realize that I had not imagined the whole thing, because what I witnessed next was enough to drive any sane person mad.

My great aunt fell in a heap not three feet from me and began to convulse. I managed to pull myself up just a little on the door frame and reached out to her. But before I could touch her spastic body, I saw that her skin was rippling across her frame as if worms writhed beneath the surface. Her hair lost its sheen and shriveled from a luscious red mane to crisp, steel-grey frizz, burnt and dry as any desert. I drew back in horror.

Maggie shook in tense, uncontrollable jerks and, with every convulsion, her youth drained away. Her breasts grew flat, her lips lost their fullness, lines and wrinkles crawled across her face like tiny snakes until they settled into furrows in her cheeks and brows. The firmness of her skin seemed to melt from underneath, leaving sags and jowls where there had been bright, plump cheeks minutes ago. Shriveling, shriveling.

I turned away from the scene and wretched on the floor for several minutes. When I was done, Great Aunt Maggie was lying in the hall, taking her breath in wheezes.

"It's...it's so beautiful!" she said, reaching a bony, arthritic finger towards the ceiling.

"Aunt Maggie!" I crawled over and brushed the grey hair from her face. "Are you..."

"I'm at peace, child. For the first time in a long time, I'm at peace. I paid a dear price, Bridget, a dear price for my secret. But, I have no secrets now. Only the truth."

"I'm not sure I can walk, Aunt Maggie.

225

Maybe I can call someone to help us."

"No need. Yeh've helped me plenty. Yer the one needin' help. I'm sorry I kept you, I'm sorry..."

"It's okay, Aunt Maggie." She looked fragile and broken, like a doll that had fallen from a high shelf. "I'll be fine."

"Yes, yes yeh will. I can see that." Her blue eyes regained their sparkle for just a moment. "They're all goin' to be just fine now. I can see...oh, it's so beautiful!" A smile broke out on her lips, she took in a deep breath, her stare fixed on some wonderful vision, and then, she was gone.

I closed the old woman's eyes and laid her head down gently. It was hard to sit up and impossible to stand so I began to crawl away, bit by bit. I hadn't gone three feet when a cool wind brushed the back of my neck and I turned to see my great aunt again, a youthful, ravishingly pretty Maggie, floating in a white form over her own body. In a mass of white curls sat a lovely comb. I looked on the floor. The comb was gone.

Maggie smiled at me. "I'll be seeing the Connors now, in their time. Right now there's nothing here to mourn. Yeh' are going to be fine, Bridget. Fine...."

*

"You'll be fine, Bridget. The doctor says you're going to be fine."

Someone was stroking my forehead. My eyes fluttered open to see Farrell hovering over me. A much more welcome sight than a banshee.

226

"Where am I?" It was a hospital room but I'd been in St. Clare's enough times by now to know it wasn't back home.

"Bryn Mawr Hospital. Your rib broke and caused some kind of internal bleeding. A little tiny hole in your lung too. But they fixed it. You're fine now. You're going to be fine." He kissed me softly. "Mike read your message late Sunday night. Clever move that Abigail's text. He called your aunt in Ireland and she gave us Maggie's address. The cops broke in and found you and....."

"Maggie's gone."

"Heart attack. Natural causes, they said."

"Yes," I was groggy but not groggy enough to think that explaining what really happened would in any way, shape, or form keep me out of the psyche ward. I collected my thoughts. "She fell. I heard her in the hall and ran to help her but I collapsed from the pain."

Farrell backed off a moment and studied my face.

"You played me with the vodka, Bran," he winked, "but you're not getting me twice. Maybe, when you get better you can tell me what really happened."

"Over disco fries?"

"Absolutely. Disco fries. Anything you want. You deserve it." He leaned over and kissed me.

"Ahem!"

Farrell wheeled around to face Dad and Michael who were standing in the doorway.

"Heeeey! Mr. Connor! Mike! Good to see you. I was just leaving." Farrell fairly pirouetted around the bed as he spoke, making for the door. He managed to bump into the one chair in the room, tripped over the pack he'd brought with him, and had reached the hall when Dad called out to him.

"Farrell!"

"It was just a little peck, Mr. Connor. I mean, I know she's sick and all and...."

"The visitor pass."

"Wha....?"

"There are only two visitors allowed in the room and you have one of the passes, Farrell." Dad rolled his eyes, the picture of forbearance.

Farrell fished around in his jacket and came up with a laminated pass that he'd somehow managed to scrunch up into a good imitation of the bathroom pass from gym class. He handed it to Dad with a "Here you go!" and bolted out.

Dad sat down on the mattress and kissed me on the forehead. "I'd hug you, darling girl, but I might break another rib!"

"Sorry we weren't here when you woke up, Bran. It was my fault. I made Dad leave so he could make his doctor appointment in Jersey." Mike fidgeted at the foot of the bed, leaning first on one leg, then the other. He looked excited. "You did it, you know!"

"Did what?"

"You broke the curse!"

"What do you mean?"

"Patrick and Sean! They're okay! They're out of the hospital. Well, Sean will be. Soon. Patrick woke up Monday morning with this tingling feeling all through his leg. When they went to change the bandages, the infection that was rotting his skin had just disappeared."

"That's great news!" I reached for Dad's hand. "And you, Dad. What did the doctor say?!"

"I'm just fine! I didn't want to go. I was afraid of more bad news, but now I'm glad your brother twisted my arm. Turned out to be a big relief. No scar tissue! Like I never even had the heart attack! Doctor said he never saw anything like it." Dad grinned, bent his elbow, and made a muscle. "Fightin' Irish!"

"And Dylan and Brian?"

"Brian won the Academic Decathlon!" Dad beamed. "That's why I let him cut classes today to come see you. He's downstairs with Dylan."

"And Sean's coming home soon?"

"Here! Let me call the hospital and you can talk with him." Mike dialed and handed me the phone.

"Hey, sis!"

"How are you doing?"

"I'm fine! They still don't know what happened." Sean relayed a story of a miraculous change, as unexplainable as Patrick's infection clearing up overnight. "They're releasing me as soon as the results of a few more tests come in."

"That's great, Sean. The luck of the Irish, huh?"

There was a bit of silence on the other end.

"Listen, sis. I heard what you did. Running off to find Maggie in Ireland. Getting yourself all banged up hunting her down in PA. I don't know how you fixed it. I'm not sure I even believe it was the curse. Maybe it was just coincidence that we all got hurt. Maybe it was luck that we all pulled through. But, thanks. Thanks for trying, for fighting for us."

I couldn't help it. Tears just started pouring out. Tiny dark spots on the cool white sheets.

Special thanks to the staff of the
National Library of Ireland